Sins of My Father

Black Brothers Series, Book One

By Lisa Cardiff

Sins of My Father

Limitless Publishing, LLC
Kailua, HI 96734
www.limitlesspublishing.com

Formatting: Limitless Publishing

ISBN-13: 978-1-68058-191-1
ISBN-10: 1-68058-191-0

Dedication

To my mom.

PROLOGUE

Archer

I lifted the remote off my desk, and pressed the back button and then play. An interview with Senator Thomas Wharton replayed for the tenth time on my TV screen.

"Have you decided whether you'll run for president next year?" the blonde with too much makeup and a condescending smile asked.

"I don't think I'll be able to say yes or no to that question before the end of the year," Senator Wharton answered. His bright white veneers shined like he was on a shoot for a toothpaste commercial instead of sitting down for a Monday morning television interview.

"So three months? Why the delay?" the woman said, pressing for information when anybody with ten brain cells knew he'd never give her the real answer. Politicians offered platitudes, not truths, and that reality was especially true of Senator Wharton.

"Right now, I'm going to focus on midterm elections, writing legislation that helps the middle-class, and celebrating the holidays with my beautiful family. Then, when the New Year rolls around, I intend to take the pulse of the country, my constituents, and my family, and make a final decision."

I pressed the pause button, staring at the flickering image of the man I had hated since I turned five years old.

"It's time to act. There's no way that man will occupy the Oval Office while I still have breath in my lungs," I said, turning to my best friend and half-brother, Knox.

We grew up in the same shitty trailer on a desolate bluff in Arizona plagued by monsoon winds. We endured a childhood under the nonexistent supervision of the same alcoholic mom with self-destructive tendencies miles long. We attended the same underprivileged and underfunded schools with torn books and battle-weary teachers. I clawed my way into Harvard, and he secured a place at the Naval Academy through a combination of hard work and letters to Senator Wharton that reeked of blackmail. When I started my company, Knox was the first person I hired, because he was the only person I would ever trust.

Knox glared at me through his black hipster glasses both of us knew he didn't need. At thirty years old, Knox was two years younger than me. With his blond hair and blue eyes, he was the light to my dark, and not just physically. Somehow, Knox made it through our childhood house of horrors and six-plus years of military service without tainting his soul. I hadn't even seen half the shit he had, and I couldn't say the same thing about myself.

"Are you sure you want to do this?" Knox plopped down into the deep cushioned, camel leather couch that stretched along the back wall of my office.

"More than anything." I reached into my desk drawer, snagging two Cuban cigars from my rosewood humidor. I clipped the ends of both cigars and held one out to him. "This calls for a celebration, don't you think?"

"No thanks. You know I can't stand the things."

"I know." I lit my cigar, took a couple puffs, and exhaled two perfect concentric rings.

"Don't you think you should let the past go?" Knox finally said, his voice low and reflective. "You have millions of dollars in the bank, homes in at least four different cities, you date beautiful women, and you have the best brother in the world." He chuckled at his attempt at making a joke. "What more could you want?"

As I slid the red and gold paper band off my cigar, I looked back at Senator Wharton's frozen image on the screen. I hated everything about that man, from his carefully groomed hair to his penchant for Ferragamo loafers, and his trademark fake smile.

Pacing around my desk, I surveyed every detail of the office I considered more of a home than the place I slept at night. Large antique walnut desk. Wood paneled walls. Looped tan carpet. Floor to ceiling windows. My corner office occupied at least five hundred prime square feet of real estate overlooking the Potomac River. I'd come a long way from a run-down trailer in the middle of the desert.

Knox was right. I had more money than I could spend in five lifetimes. I had power, influence, name recognition, and every material thing imaginable at my fingertips, but I hadn't achieved the one thing that had fueled my desire for success over the last twenty-seven years.

"Revenge. I want revenge," I pointed at the TV screen, "that ends with the complete and utter destruction of that man and every person in his life."

"Are you sure you want to do this? It will change everything."

"I've never been more certain of anything in my life." It was the absolute truth. Every decision in my life had been made with this moment in mind.

Knox sighed and propped his gray chukka clad feet on the circular glass coffee table. "I don't understand it, but if it's what you want, I'm all in. I'll help any way I can."

CHAPTER ONE

Langley

"Is it possible to have fun at these parties?" A warm, velvety voice mixed with a hint of steel washed over my body, causing the hair on my arms to stand at attention.

Reluctantly, I looked up from my phone. Dark glossy hair, even darker eyes, heavily stubbled jaw line—but in a perfectly groomed sort of way— chiseled even features, broad shoulders, and a narrow waist, all wrapped up in a black suit that managed to be both professional and sinful. I hadn't seen him at one of these parties before. He must have been new to this scene, and by scene I meant the political cesspool of D.C.

My mom married the distinguished Senator Thomas Wharton from Arizona when I was twelve, and I successfully evaded these parties for four years until his advisors decided I was an asset to his image. Now, I was veteran. I'd been coming to these things for eight years. Each one was infinitely more painful than the last.

Like a worthless spectator, I watched people blow smoke up my stepdad's ass and funnel shady money into even shadier black holes over and over, night after night, until any faith I had in our political system evaporated. Politics in action didn't resemble the lofty principles touted by my high school civics teacher. Not even close. In fact, it reminded me of the smoky, backroom deals crafted in mafia movies.

"It depends on your idea of fun," I answered dryly. I briefly met his chocolate eyes before returning my attention to the increasingly heated texts between my best friend Winnie and me. She promised she'd come to the fundraiser tonight, but she ditched me to go to some new club. I was mad, but I didn't blame her. If I had anything resembling a backbone, I wouldn't subject myself to these parties either.

"Is this your idea of fun?" he asked, leaning against the wall and crossing his ankles, an amused smile dancing at the corners of his lush mouth. An annoying jolt of adrenaline flooded my veins. The way his lips curled up at the corners as though he knew my most embarrassing secret almost made me blush.

"Isn't it yours?" I retorted, evading his too intense stare. He probably thought I could introduce him to my stepdad. It wouldn't happen. We spoke on an as-needed basis. When I visited, we passed each other in the halls of his D.C. townhouse barely acknowledging each other. In public, it was another story. He pretended we were the perfect family, but

I didn't care. It could be worse. I could have Winnie's parents. I'd take indifference over active disdain any day of the week.

"No." He paused and then cocked his head to the side, his gaze hooded. "I can think of a million better ways to spend a Friday night."

His dark hair tickled the collar of his pressed white dress shirt. My fingers itched to touch the inky strands to see if they were as silky as they looked. I groaned inwardly. I needed to get a hold of my stupid emotions. This was a stuffy political fundraiser, not a speed dating event or a bar.

I stuffed my phone into my black clutch. "Then why are you here?"

"I was invited."

"Lucky you," I answered with a subtle trace of sarcasm. I painted a bright smile on my face to dampen the effect. I never wanted to piss someone off too much, especially someone I didn't know. You never knew when that person might be useful to the Wharton political machine. While I hated everything about that ruthless machine, I decided long ago to go along for the ride rather than buck the tide. As much as I'd love to be the modern day David and take down Goliath, I didn't believe I was the person to do the job, so I pushed all my conflicting emotions out of my mind long ago. It'd been incredibly easy. Too easy.

"Maybe." His eyes drifted from my mouth down my body, pausing on the chest of my fitted, standard issue black cocktail dress. By standard issue, I didn't mean boring. The designer dress hugged my curvy body in all the right places, but it was understated enough not to ruffle the feathers of my stepdad's political advisors, yet feminine enough to satisfy my mom's not so subtle desire for me to land a powerful husband. I had at least twenty similar dresses in my closet selected and approved by my stepdad's advisors who never overlooked an opportunity, no matter how small, to manipulate public opinion.

His lips curled into a cocky smile that managed to piss me off even more. "I'm Archer." He held out his hand, but I didn't acknowledge the gesture.

Except for the two of us, the gilded-wood paneled Georgian-inspired hallway was empty, which meant I didn't need to feign interest in him or anyone else at that second. In my opinion, the hallway was a safe zone, kind of like seeking sanctuary in a church in the middle ages.

"Thanks for sharing," I responded.

"In polite conversation, it's custom to shake my hand and offer your name in return." He cocked one eyebrow, reminding me how much I hated the gesture. My stepfather used it on half the world—myself included—to express his contempt and overall condescension for any idea except his own.

I raised my eyebrows and folded my arms across my chest. "Is that what this is?"

He tapped his fingers on the wall behind him. "I'd like it to be."

"That's too bad, because I've met my quota of polite conversation today." I tilted my head to the side as though I were contemplating my words. "Actually, I've met my quota for the entire year. Find someone who's interested in indulging in shallow, meaningless conversation." I flung my arm toward the door of the ballroom. "There's a whole room full of people in there spewing disingenuous words and insincere platitudes like confetti. You're free to join them."

He chuckled. The sound of his deep, masculine laugh did foolish things to my heart and sent my synapses into overdrive. Shit. I didn't want my body to react to this man, or any man remotely connected to my stepdad. If either my mom or my stepdad suspected I harbored any interest in a man in their circle of associates, they'd start inventing reasons to shove him in my face. Trust me, it happened in the past, and it ended badly. Even if this man was the exception, being connected to my stepdad was an automatic black mark in my mind.

"I'd prefer to talk to someone I don't know," he answered with a courteous look on his face.

I rolled my fingers over the individual nubs of my two-tiered pearl necklace, squeezing each one harder than necessary. "Are you saying you don't know who I am?" I didn't mean to act like a pompous bitch, but everybody who was anyone knew who I was, or at least at these events and in these elite political circles.

His lips quivered, but he brushed his hands over his mouth to conceal his reaction. "Right. You're Senator Wharton's daughter, but I usually like to start a conversation with an introduction, some small talk, and then who knows..." His voice trailed off, and he popped the button on his suit jacket, fingering something in his pocket. A flask? A phone? You could never tell at these events. If I could hide a flask in my bra, I would've done it. My stepdad's spies counted my drinks at these events, not that I had a problem. It was one of many preventative measures to ensure no unsavory events occurred, which might overshadow the purpose of the evening.

"Stepdaughter," I snapped before I could stop myself. I hated that everyone conveniently dropped the "step" from my relationship with Senator Wharton. I had a dad. He died when I was ten years old, but that didn't mean I wanted to wipe him from my memory and forget his blood ran through my veins. My mother may have dumped his name and tried to erase him from our collective memories, but I wouldn't forget. I loved him, all of him, even his faults. He was real in a way my stepdad could never be, and that said a lot considering my dad's occupation and the circumstances surrounding his death.

He shoved his hand through his slightly wavy, dark hair. "He didn't adopt you?"

"No." I didn't need to answer the question. It wasn't his business, but I hated when people assumed he had adopted me. I didn't want him to be my father. Except for giving me shelter and food, he didn't raise me. I couldn't even say he cared about me with any degree of certainty.

He nodded, his eyes examining me, and I prayed to whoever cared that I managed to keep my face neutral and scrubbed of any emotion. I didn't need my lukewarm, sometimes cold relationship with Senator Wharton to become common knowledge. It'd hurt my mom, and it'd send my stepdad's political advisors into a tizzy. I didn't need another session with his PR team to coach me how to behave in public, especially now that my stepdad had hired an exploratory committee to determine whether he should run for president. I expected him to announce his candidacy by the end of the month. His political advisors already emailed me a weekly briefing containing my schedule and talking points.

Janis Joplin's "Piece of My Heart" blared from my phone, and the tension tugging at my muscles released ever so slightly. The song was my anthem these days as I let my stepdad's life steal a little bit of my soul day by day.

"Nice ringtone."

I pulled the phone out of my purse. "It's my alarm."

"For what?"

I smiled as I turned off the alarm. "To leave."

"I'll walk you out." He pushed his body away from the wall and held out his arm in some antiquated gentlemanly gesture that would be endearing if I were interested in him. I wasn't. His sexy smile and even sexier swagger didn't do anything for me. Well, not anything I'd admit to any living creature, including myself.

"No thanks." I breezed by him. I had no intention of taking his arm or touching him. I didn't know anything about him except his name. With as many secrets as my family had, I couldn't trust strangers, and I didn't want anything to do with Archer.

Okay...maybe I exaggerated. There was a split second there where I imagined him stripped of his black suit, white starched shirt, and emerald and charcoal striped tie, his obviously broad shoulders and narrow waist exposed. Something about him made me crave really stupid things... like licking the side of his neck or biting his delicious lower lip. If I were anyone else, I might have indulged in the impulse, but I couldn't. I was Langley Mayer, ice queen, daughter of the late actor Rick Mayer, and prop for Senator Wharton's nonexistent compassionate side, which meant I wouldn't do a damn thing.

My red heels echoed off the walls as I breezed down the marble-tiled hallway, eating up the space between the exit and me one click at a time. Unfortunately, I heard the leather-soled shuffle of Archer's shoes following me. If I made it to the front doors, taxis would be lined up next to the curb. I could slide in the backseat of one before I had to exchange another word with him. I couldn't take my parents' chauffeured car because I didn't want the driver to report my comings and goings to my mom.

Three steps before I reached the double glass doors, Archer darted forward and pushed it open for me. I paused, and he arched his eyebrows, daring me to do what? Ignore him? Reverse my course and go back to the party? Like someone had just suggested I scrape my nails over a chalkboard, I shivered at the thought of returning to the party. I didn't know how much longer I could successfully avoid Brandon. Turning back wasn't an option.

I backpedaled a few feeble steps. Archer's jaw tightened, and his formerly warm chocolate eyes darkened. As my mind contemplated my next move,

I spotted a few photographers waiting at the end of the walkway. I wasn't famous…not by any stretch of my imagination, but my photo did occasionally appear in newspaper and website gossip columns. I hated it. They discussed my stepdad's political career. They speculated on my real dad's drug overdose, which meant references to whether I'd follow in his self-destructive footsteps.

I did the only thing I could do to avoid unwanted attention. I sauntered out of the building, head held high, shoulders squared, and a not quite sincere smile cracking the corners of my mouth.

"Thank you," I said, tipping my head to Archer.

Within seconds, he closed the space between us, and his hand connected with my lower back. The heat from the palm of his hand scorched the silk blend of my dress, stealing my breath and setting my body on fire.

Of their own volition and entirely without my permission, my eyes locked on his, and a breezy, almost nonexistent tremor journeyed the length of my spine. The lopsided grin on his face told me without words that my reaction to his touch didn't go unnoticed. I bit back a sharp retort as bulbs flashed in my face, capturing the moment. Great, just what I wanted to avoid.

He opened the back door of the first available taxi and signaled for me to enter with an elegant sweep of his hand. As I leaned forward to tell the driver my destination, Archer slipped into the backseat beside me.

"The Lux," he said.

"Wait. What?" My mind whirled. How did he

know my destination? Did he plan to go with me?

He pulled the door closed. "We're going to the same place. We might as well share the cab."

My eyes landed on his mouth for at least the fifth time in the last twenty minutes. Breaking the trance, I jerked my gaze to small scratches on the Plexiglas separating us from the driver. Slowly, I scooted across the seat, pressing my body against the sticky, duct taped vinyl on the inside of the opposite door. "You're freaking me out. How do you know I'm going there?"

"I might have inadvertently seen the text message exchange." He rested his arm along the back of the seat. My gaze zeroed in on the favorable stretch of his white shirt over his obviously muscular chest. My heart did this funky double beat thing that made me catch my breath. Ugh. Could I be any more cliché?

"So you decided to accompany me?"

"I'm meeting someone there."

I folded my arms across my chest. "And you expect me to believe that?"

"It's the truth."

"Right." I lifted my phone and snapped a picture of him in profile.

"What's that for?" he asked.

"I'm sending it to my friend in case I never make it to the bar," I said without looking up from my phone. "You can never be too careful."

He didn't answer, so I stared out the window. Tall narrow buildings lined the streets. Restaurant outdoor patios overflowed with people. Trees dotted the sidewalks in even intervals.

Like any Friday night in this town, traffic crawled. I didn't need to look at the speedometer to know the cab's average speed hovered between ten and fifteen miles per hour. Every second and mile between the stuffy fundraiser lightened my mood, so I didn't complain. I needed to say no to those events more often.

His phone rang, that annoying old car horn ringtone. It went on and on.

Honk.

Honk.

Honk.

I shifted awkwardly in my seat. "Aren't you going to answer that?"

"No."

"You're not even going to look who's calling? What if it's an emergency?"

"It's not."

"You don't know that." I toyed with my necklace, twisting it back and forth.

He leaned toward me, and his shoulder brushed against mine. "I like living dangerously. I'll take the chance," he said casually, a prince charming smile spreading across his face. I think his eyes even twinkled. "Besides, it's rude to take a call while you're with someone." He waved his hand back and forth as though he needed to clarify he was with me.

"I don't mind."

"You should." He paused, his warm chocolaty eyes studying me, weighing me. What did he see? "You deserve more than bits and pieces of someone's attention."

"Thank you," I said for a lack of anything else to

say. Since I'd broken up with my ex six months ago, my ego had been in the dumps. Don't get me wrong—I didn't miss him, but the timing sucked. In three months, I'd turn twenty-five, and my mom didn't let one chance slip away without reminding me that I was approaching the downward slide to my thirties. Accordingly to her, being single at thirty wasn't acceptable, a total failure in her mind. I didn't agree. Thirty was the new twenty, but her words made me feel deficient.

The taxi stopped in front of The Lux. A black awning shadowed the dark glass doors marking the entrance. To the right, people lounged at small round tables enclosed by a frosted waist height fence.

"We're here," I mumbled to myself.

Before I opened my purse, Archer paid the driver and slipped out the door. He waited until I exited and closed the door behind me.

"It was nice to meet you, Langley Wharton."

Without waiting for a response, he moved toward the entrance to The Lux. A dark-haired woman in a wispy blue dress lifted her hand, a huge smile spreading her blood-red lips across her face. He draped an arm around her waist, resting his hand on her hip as he guided her into the bar. I felt dowdy in comparison with my simple black dress and neutral makeup.

I halted mid-step on the sidewalk, barely able to move. He hadn't lied. He really planned to meet someone here. He wasn't interested in me. Relief and loss collided inside of my chest.

Just as he reached the rectangular concrete

planter next to the entrance, he glanced over his shoulder, his eyes totally unreadable, and I finally managed to shut my mouth and suppress the disappointment pumping through my veins. The wind rippled through the still bare limbs of the cherry trees lining the sidewalk, whipping my hair around my face. Spring hadn't arrived, and I needed to get inside before I froze. I didn't wear a jacket. Damn my vanity.

CHAPTER TWO

Langley

"Winnie," I said, leaning over and tapping her on the shoulder.

"Hey, Langley." She lifted her purse from the empty chair next to her. "Sit. I saved you a seat."

"Is that your way of seeking forgiveness for ditching the fundraiser earlier tonight?"

She groaned and flipped her white blonde hair over her shoulder. "I'm sorry. I just can't go to another one of those. I'm totally fried. If I'm forced to have another conversation about the pros and cons of hydraulic fracturing, I'll lose my mind."

I perched on the stool, crossing my ankles, hooking one heel inside the metal footrest and resting one elbow on the mahogany slab counter. "I know, and that's exactly why I should hate you for making me to fend for myself without an escape route."

"Don't go next time. You're twenty-four. You have your own career, your own life, and your own money. You don't have to jump when they ask."

"It's complicated," I answered, twirling a piece of my not quite blonde, not quite brown hair around my finger, tighter and tighter with each turn.

Winnie yanked my fingers out of my hair. "No, there's nothing complicated about living your life on your terms. You have a great job as a physical therapist—"

"Not so great according to my mom."

Winnie rolled her eyes. "What does your mom know? She's never worked a day in her life."

"And she doesn't think I need to work either. But if I insist on working, she thinks it should be a job with a charitable purpose." I lifted a hand signaling for the bartender. I needed a drink.

"Why do you care what she thinks?" She lifted a glass of wine to her lips.

"I don't."

Winnie choked on the drink before covering her mouth with her hand. "If you didn't care, you wouldn't bend over backward to attend those stupid fundraisers. You can go to the big ones, but you need to concentrate on your career goals, not your stepdad's."

I rubbed my temples. I wish it were as simple as Winnie made it sound. I'd love to find a way to extricate myself from the Wharton political machine without causing a major rift between my mom and me. She wasn't the best mom, but she was the only family I had. "If it were any other time, I would do it."

"It's never going to be the right time for them, but it is the right time for you."

"I know. I know." And I did, but that didn't make severing the ties any easier.

The bartender slid a napkin in front of me. "What do you want to drink?"

"A house pinot grigio." I didn't like white wine. I preferred red wine, but even one glass made my head hurt the next day, so I settled for my second choice like so many other things in my life.

"Sure thing," he said.

"Cheers." I lifted my glass and held it up in front of Winnie.

"Cheers."

Winnie tapped her glass against mine and drained the rest of her wine. I took a sip, savoring the subtle pear flavor as it rolled over my tongue.

"So." Winnie leaned forward, resting her elbow on the counter. "Was it as bad as I thought it'd be?"

I chuckled. "Exactly that bad." I angled my chin to the side. "But I met someone."

Winnie's eyes widened. "Please tell me your mom didn't try to set you up with another one of your stepdad's staff members or a stuffy old donor with deep pockets and even deeper wrinkles."

"No." A wave of revulsion rippled down my spine. Last year, my mom set me up with one of my stepdad's senior staffers, Brandon. At first, I was excited. Brandon seemed perfect, from his groomed looks to his vocal support of my career choice. But after six months, our relationship exploded in my face and ended really ugly. Like most people in political circles, he valued a win more than a moral outcome. Sadly, he still worked for my stepdad, and I saw him all the time.

"I met him in the foyer on my way out of the fundraiser. We chatted and shared a taxi here." My fingers fidgeted with the hem of my dress, and I crossed and uncrossed my legs a couple times. Why did the thought of Archer make me nervous...on edge?

"So where is he?" Winnie glanced over her shoulder, her eyes not so subtly scanning the people.

I shrugged. "I don't know. He met his date at the door. Tall, elegant brunette. End of the story. Nothing to share."

Winnie slapped my shoulder playfully. "You suck. I thought you meant you shared numbers, or made plans, or anything."

I smirked. "I know. I wanted you to think you missed something other than two hours of unremarkable, mind-numbing conversation."

"I won't hold my breath." Winnie squealed like a six year old on a swing and squeezed my arm, her light pink fingernails scraping the tender skin on the inside of my forearm. "Oh my God! Was that him in the picture you texted me?"

"Yes."

"Now I am jealous. Too bad he shared and dashed."

My brows furrowed. "What the hell are you talking about?"

"You know, like dine and dash." When I didn't respond, she rolled her eyes. "You're such a prude sometimes. You know...dine and ditch. Eat and Run. Chew and Screw. He shared a taxi, then took off."

I laughed. "I know what you're talking about, but your analogy wasn't funny."

"Ugh." Winnie pulled a twenty-dollar bill out of her purse. "Here." She dangled it between her thumb and her index finger. "Order me another glass of wine. I need to go to the bathroom. I've been saving our seats for forty minutes, and my bladder is going to explode any second."

"Go." I waved her money away. "Your drink is on me."

"Thanks," she said, sliding off the stool. "I'll buy the next round." She tapped her lips. "Unless your knight in shining armor dumps his date for you."

A twinge of pain zipped through my chest, but I told myself it didn't mean anything. I'd never see Archer again. "Not likely."

"You never know," she said, smiling before she left me at the bar by myself.

I twisted the wineglass by the stem on the counter, trying to avoid making eye contact with anyone. Talking to strangers at a bar wasn't my thing. I didn't mind going for drinks or even dancing with friends, but unlike some of my friends, I didn't go out to look for men. I preferred to date men I met through mutual friends or my co-workers.

Two hands dropped on my shoulders. "Is that seat taken?"

I groaned. I didn't have to turn around to know Brandon stood behind me. If there were a voice lineup, I'd be able to recognize him blindfolded. His voice sounded like his words originated in his nose instead of his throat, plus he smelled as though he bathed in sandalwood. God, I hated talking to him. I hated him. Why did I waste six months of my life on him? I had successfully avoided him at the fundraiser, but apparently, he followed me here.

"Most definitely," I snapped, snagging my black clutch from the counter and slamming it on Winnie's empty seat.

In his trademarked asshole way, Brandon didn't take the hint that I didn't want to talk to him tonight or ever. I wasn't surprised. Six months of hints failed to register in his mind. Intentionally oblivious, he slid between my stool and Winnie's vacant seat, resting one elbow on the polished counter.

"You didn't stay long tonight." He toyed with the middle button of his black suit jacket, his eyes darting around the bar.

I took a longer than necessary sip of my wine. "Neither did you."

He cocked his head to the side and smirked. "I wanted to talk to you, but like clockwork, you disappeared after two hours."

"What I do isn't your concern." I folded my hands in my lap. "We don't have anything to talk about." '

"Come on, Langley." He pushed my hair behind my shoulder.

I flinched and then slapped his hand away. "Don't touch me." My stomach rolled. I dated this man for six months. His hands had touched my body. His lips had kissed mine. A shiver of disgust trickled down my spine.

I didn't hate many people in life, but I hated

Brandon. If only I'd never met him. If only I'd broken up with him when I wanted to instead of going on one more date, which turned into six months of my life. If only I hadn't picked up Brandon's iPad instead mine, I'd still be blissfully unaware and charmed in my picture-perfect life. God, I was an idiot. Why didn't I trust my instincts?

"Don't be like that." He snatched my hand out of my lap.

I glared at him. "Brandon, what do you want? Why did you follow me here?"

He leaned toward me, his nearly colorless eyes even blanker than I recalled. Tiny beads of sweat dampened his brow as he tightened his hold on my hand until the tips of my fingers tingled, protesting the lack of blood flow, and my knuckles ground against each other. "I want to know what you told Senator Wharton."

"Nothing." I wasn't lying. If I wanted, I could've said a lot of things to rattle my stepdad's life, but I didn't. Experience taught me to stay out of my stepdad's business.

The more interest I showed in what he did, the more he managed to suck me into his orbit, and I didn't want to be any closer than I already was to the inner circle of the Wharton political machine. As long as I still had the option of turning a blind eye to the less than pristine side of politics and pretending politicians had benevolent motives and moral intentions, I'd take it.

"Did you confront him or let something slip?"

I chewed on my lower lip, my mind wildly racing through the conversations I had with my stepdad in the last six months. "No."

He twisted my hand to the side, and my wrist bellowed in protest. "Don't toy with me. Think harder. I know you said something. What about your mom? Did you say something to her?"

Tears swelled in the corners of my eyes. I was about to cry. Damn it. Brandon didn't deserve my tears. "What the hell, Brandon? What's wrong with you?" I slammed my open palm against his chest, and a jolt of pain shot up my arm. "Let me go."

"Not until you tell me what you told Senator Wharton." His voice was dead and stagnant with anger.

"That you're an asshole!" I snarled through my teeth as I shoved his chest again. "Leave me alone or I'll spill the information in that email to anyone who will listen. I haven't breathed a word in six months, not even to my mom, but that could change the minute I get home tonight. Maybe I'll start by confronting Senator Wharton, or I'll go directly to the—"

"You bitch," he spat, yanking me off the stool, pulling my body flush against his. "You don't understand how bad this could get for the both of us. We will be fucked!"

CHAPTER THREE

Archer

I had watched as Brandon approached Langley. I knew I needed to give her some space and concentrate on the woman sitting across from me, but I couldn't resist the compulsion to stare at her. My greedy gaze drank her in. Her clothes were classy and nondescript, but she didn't need any adornment. Cat-like green eyes, full dark pink lips, and perfectly etched cheekbones made everything else superfluous.

Maybe it was a trick of the light, but she glowed as though she had a spotlight shining down on her, highlighting her caramel-colored hair. Illusion or not, Langley was a hundred times more beautiful in person than in pictures I'd been reviewing over the last few months.

And her voice...

When she first opened her mouth at the fundraiser, her raspy tone reminded me of smoky whiskey and hot nights. She wasn't like any of the women, past or present, in my life, and I wanted her, which was an unfortunate complication. She was also the woman I intended to use to take down Senator Wharton.

Several graphic and wholly inappropriate ideas popped into my head when she asked if the fundraiser was my idea of fun. Wisely, I didn't give voice to them. At first, I had believed she wasn't interested in me, but she had too studiously avoided eye contact with me outside the fundraiser and in the taxi for that. No, contrary to what she wanted me to think, she was very aware of me. Even now in the bar, I didn't miss the not so coincidental glances over her shoulder in my direction. I intended to use her curiosity to my benefit.

According to my research on the Wharton family, Brandon and Langley had dated for six months, and everyone expected them to get married. On paper and in person, they painted a pretty picture. Langley had caramel-colored hair, yellowish-green eyes, and a magazine worthy sophisticated style. Brandon had pretty boy looks, a Harvard law degree, and a noteworthy future in politics. He made the ideal successor to the Wharton political machine.

For undiscoverable reasons, their relationship ended suddenly. None of my contacts found any information to explain it.

No cheating.

No fighting.

No lying.

Nothing…at least on the surface, or anything either party had documented in email or texts.

To anyone not paying attention, it appeared the relationship ended amicably, but I had spent my entire life reading between the lines, and everything between the lines said there was more to their story.

Tonight, like every other fundraiser with both of them in attendance, Langley went to extremes to avoid interacting with Brandon or ending up in the same circle of conversation. Bathroom breaks. Hiding in the hallway. Hovering near the buffet table. Langley had perfected the art of dodging anything and everything related to Brandon.

Her body language validated my instinct that there was bad blood between them. When Brandon's hand circled hers, and Langley winced in pain, I found the opportunity I needed to intervene.

Within seconds, I was on my feet and across the bar. I grabbed Brandon's forearm, squeezing until he released her from his grasp. "Back off. She doesn't want to be touched."

Langley's head snapped to the side. "Archer?"

Brandon pressed a finger against my chest. "This is none of your business. Walk away."

"I'm making it my business." With narrowed eyes, I stared at the finger he planted in the center of my chest for a split second before I grabbed it and twisted it just as he had twisted Langley's wrist thirty seconds earlier. Brandon squirmed and wiggled until he broke my hold. He was lucky I didn't break his finger. I didn't let people touch me without my consent. Ever. Growing up in a trailer park, I learned fast that if you didn't retaliate, you ended up bullied or hurt, and I refused to allow a self-important ass like Brandon bully me.

"Archer." Langley scooped up her clutch from the empty stool. "I'm fine now. Don't let Brandon drag you into a fight. He's not worth it."

"Who's he? Are you dating him now?" Brandon sneered, his chest heaving and the veins along the side of his neck bulging. "You left the fundraiser with him too."

"My life isn't your business." Langley flipped her hair over her shoulder and tipped up her chin. To an outsider, she looked composed and confident, but her fingers shook as she white-knuckled her purse.

Folding my arms across my chest and raising one eyebrow, I didn't offer any additional information. He could come to his own conclusion. If he thought we were together, I was one baby step closer to where I needed to be.

Brandon interlaced his fingers and flexed them toward his chest as he stared down his nose at me. A good three inches shorter than me, his intimidation technique failed. I stifled a laugh.

"Don't waste your time on Langley. You'd think with Rick Mayer for a dad that she'd know how to have fun. Oh no. She's more frigid and boring than any woman I've ever met, and that's saying a lot considering all the women in D.C. are vanilla carbon copies."

"Then you shouldn't have any problem leaving Langley alone," I said, my jaw clenched tight. I didn't know much information about Brandon other than his connection to Langley and Senator Wharton, but I'd encountered his type at Harvard and in the financial world often. Entitled. Self-important. Pretentious. I wrapped my arm around her shoulder and pulled her close to my side, shielding her from his poisonous glare.

Brandon shoved his hand into his gelled hair and then held his hands out wide. "I'd be happy to as long as she keeps her end of our bargain."

Langley licked her raspberry-stained lower lip. "I already told you I have. You don't have any reason to believe otherwise. If I change my mind, you'll be the first to know."

Brandon nodded and his shoulders slumped, as though her words alone had robbed him of his argument.

"You heard her." With Langley still wrapped in my embrace, I stepped forward, pushing past him. Brandon stumbled backward a step or two, barely catching his balance before he tripped over the barstool.

I kept walking, threading our joined bodies through the crowd swaying back and forth in excited waves. She didn't say a word until I reached the door.

She halted. "Wait," she demanded, her voice raspier than usual. "I'm not leaving with you."

"Why not? We came here together." Technically, it was true, but just like right now, I had manipulated my way into the taxi with her.

In one silken move, she liberated her curvy body from my embrace. "I'm here with Winnie. I can't just disappear without saying something. She'll be worried."

"So text her."

Her mouth opened and closed in quick

succession. Then, she folded her arms across her chest, holding her purse in front of her breastbone like a shield. "What about your date?"

I groaned inwardly. Desperate to get Langley away from Brandon, I had left Leah alone at our table without a word. Generally, Leah didn't care what I did as long as I apologized later with a gift or a dinner. My money and my connections were all she wanted from me anyway, but that didn't make her a bad person. She never lied about her expectations, and I didn't lie about mine. I admired her honesty and her wicked sense of humor about the whole arrangement. Her past made her incapable of more, and I respected her for being up front about it.

"I'll text her. She'll live." And she would. She'd find someone else within the hour. Leah was resourceful. She didn't waste opportunities, and neither did I, and in order for my plan to work, I needed Langley.

"We aren't friends. You don't know me." She pinched the bridge of her nose. "I don't get it. Why are you helping me?"

"Because you look like you needed help," I said, answering her as simply as possible. The real reason for my interest in her was a maze of perverse and convoluted turns, but she didn't need to know about any of that...yet.

She took a step backward and planted both of her hands on her hips. "Lots of people need help."

"Fair enough." I smiled. "I'd like to get to know you. You're beautiful. You're smart, and you're interesting, or least that's my first impression of you. Stop overthinking my motives."

"And I'm related to Senator Wharton."

"There's that, but I'm not so sure that's a good thing."

She gave me a wary look, her forehead crinkling and the corner of her lips curling downward. "You'd be the first to believe that."

"And that's why you should trust me."

She scoffed and rolled her eyes. "Oh please."

"It's a taxi ride, not a marriage proposal." I held out my hand, urging her to come with me.

"Just a taxi ride? Nothing else."

"If I'm lucky, maybe you'll agree to meet me for lunch or dinner sometime. If not," I shrugged, "then we'll both move on with our lives, exchanging meaningless greetings if we run into each other in the future."

Langley's shoulders sagged, and her eyes darted to the side. "Fine. I don't want to stay anyway. I can't take another confrontation with Brandon tonight, but I'm not promising anything."

Perfect. Mission accomplished. I grabbed her hand and pulled her toward the exit. "Then, let's get out of here."

CHAPTER FOUR

Langley

Inside the cab, I immediately cracked the window. It smelled like cigarette smoke. I didn't think you could smoke in a cab, but apparently, people did, or this driver did, and he tried to cover it up with a pine scented air freshener shaped like a Christmas tree dangling from the rear-view mirror. Instead of masking the odor, it reminded me of the smell of my hair the night after sitting around a campfire.

"So what's that guy's story?" Archer said as the cab darted into traffic.

"Brandon?" I said. I tapped my fingers on my leg, fighting the exhaustion settling in the pit of my stomach. I didn't want to talk about Brandon for so many reasons, but mostly because our baggage was not something to be shared in a ten-minute taxi ride with a stranger, or even your best friend. Brandon and my stepdad killed a piece of my soul and stole any innocent illusions I still harbored about life and my family, in particular.

"Yes. Brandon."

He grinned at me, flashing his perfectly aligned white teeth. Just that simple gesture was like a lightning bolt, snapping me out of my maudlin mood. An unexpected excitement buzzed through my veins like I was on the verge of something new. Thrilling. Life altering. What the hell? I promised I'd never get involved with anyone connected to my stepdad again, which meant Archer embodied everything I didn't want in my life right now.

Sexy. Magnetic. Connected to my stepdad. Involved with another woman or women. The elegant brunette could be one of many in the Rolodex of a sexy, well-connected and visibly wealthy man like Archer.

"Long story," I said, my words clipped. Brandon seemed uncharacteristically edgy tonight. Normally, even the worst news didn't faze him. That's why he earned the position as my stepdad's right-hand man.

To my undying relief, Archer nodded instead of pushing the subject.

"So how do you know Senator Wharton?" I asked, trying to change the trajectory of our conversation and drill the necessity for distance into my brain. Being acquainted with my stepdad was the new meter I used to judge whether I wanted anything to do with someone.

"I don't." He cleared his throat. "Not socially anyway. We've never spoken at length."

"But you said you were invited to the fundraiser tonight."

"I was."

I adjusted the hem of my dress. "Do we need to play twenty questions before I can pull the answer out of you?"

"I own a financial management firm, Black Investments. I think your stepdad is interested in the depth of my pockets. On a personal level, he doesn't give a shit about me. I didn't even talk to him tonight."

"Black Investments," I said, nodding my head. Holy shit. Black Investments was a big fucking deal. "You're that Archer Black." This man was a legend in the financial industry. I'm not in the financial industry, but I read the financial section of the newspaper on occasion, and his investment strategy or opinion was newsworthy in and of itself. I couldn't count the number of times I read an article about him or the insane returns he earned for his clients. Even crazier, he only accepted clients with a net worth that exceeded two hundred million. "Wow. That's a big deal." I rubbed my hand over my lips.

He smirked, but unlike his other smiles, he didn't look amused. "Did I finally manage to impress you?"

"Yes. I mean no. Is there a right answer?" I didn't want him to think his financial status changed my mind about him. Obviously, I was impressed. Who wouldn't be? His life was a classic rags to riches story. Born to a teenage mother, who, according to the trashier tabloids, was a former prostitute, he grew up in a trailer park. Somehow he managed to snag a full ride scholarship to Harvard. When he graduated, he worked as an options trader for a few years. Then, he formed his own financial firm. The rest was history.

"Most people are impressed with my financial status, but I'd like to think there are other reasons to be impressed," he answered, the harsh lines of his face softening faintly.

I smiled and squeezed him arm. "Like your good looks."

"Yes." He chuckled as his leg nudged mine. "There's that. I'm glad you noticed."

"Did you decide whether to donate?" I asked, ignoring the desire coursing like wildfire through my body every single time we touched.

I needed to concentrate on the facts. Archer had the kind of money that made my stepdad's political operatives swarm like sharks in bloodied water. That meant my stepdad and my mom would push me to use my connection to him…not that it was much of a connection. We shared a taxi twice, and he saved me from Brandon's verbal lashing. Beyond that, I probably wouldn't see him again. Was that disappointment twisting my stomach into knots, or just the wine hitting my empty stomach like an acid bomb?

"I did," he answered, lowering his voice.

My mouth puckered like I sucked on a sour lemon. "So you're going to do it?"

"Shouldn't I be having this conversation with Senator Wharton's political team, or are you interested in shaking me down for money too?"

"No. I don't care about raising money. I don't like spending time with people involved in business or otherwise with my stepdad." My relationship with Brandon taught me to stay far away from my stepdad's spidery fingers.

"Why not?"

My lungs inflated with air as I sucked in a breath, deliberating what I wanted to reveal. "Brandon is my ex and he still works for my stepdad. It didn't end well. I don't want to go there again."

"So does that mean you're thinking about seeing me again?" His large hand rubbed the length of his jaw, then he dropped his hand back into his lap.

"I...I don't know." I didn't know how to respond. If I denied it, it'd be a lie. I did want to see him again, and not because of his wealth or influence, but because I liked talking to him. I liked how easily he defused the situation with Brandon. I liked that he offered to ride home with me.

Turning to the side, he met my frazzled stare. His fingertip trailed from my shoulder to my wrist. Even though his touch was ethereal and almost nonexistent, it ignited every nerve ending in its wake. "You don't know, or you're not interested? Either way, you don't need to soften the blow. I'm a big boy. I'll accept your answer, whatever it is, graciously."

I chewed on my lip, my mind swirling like an odds maker in Vegas, calculating the pros and cons of letting Archer into my life. "I don't know if I'm ready for anything."

"Not even a no strings exploratory coffee or lunch date?"

"Maybe that'd be okay," I hedged. What was wrong with spending an hour or two more with

Archer? Nothing, right? I hated that my life had come to evaluating people based on their connection to my stepdad, but after what I learned about him, I couldn't stand being in his sphere of influence.

The taxi pulled to the curb, idling in front of my small two-bedroom townhome in Georgetown that I rented from my stepdad. It had broad front steps with a gray wood railing and a black metal roof portico. I loved everything about the townhome, from its narrow wooden stairs to the second story, and its ornate carved wood fireplaces in every room. At that second, I wished I lived outside of D.C. so I had a few more minutes with Archer.

"If it makes any difference, I'm not going to commit any money to Senator Wharton's campaign."

I cracked the door open. "Now or never?"

"Never is a long time, but I don't plan to donate any money."

I tilted my head to the side. "Why? You don't share his political beliefs?"

"Something like that." He knocked on the Plexiglas window. "Give me five minutes and I'll be back."

I stepped out of the car. "You don't have to walk me to the door. I'm good."

"I'm not. What kind of man would I be if I didn't walk a woman to her door at night?"

"A normal one." I glanced over my shoulder as I walked to my front door.

"Then you haven't been hanging out with the right kind of men." His hand pressed into my lower back again, guiding me up the steps. Shit. My skin tingled under his splayed fingertips.

"Obviously." I snorted. "I can't dispute that point after what happened with Brandon tonight."

His hand slid around my back to my hip as we reached my front door. He squeezed it and then released his hold on me, but he still hovered inches from my body. His presence fogged my brain. Why did I have to be attracted to this man? Why not Todd, my coworker, or someone equally innocuous and predictable? Life wasn't fair. That's why.

"Thanks for tonight. For the taxi rides. For helping me with Brandon. Everything really," I mumbled as my hand blindly fished inside of my purse for my keys—back and forth and in circles. Who would have thought finding one key in a purse with a phone and tube of lipstick could be so difficult? My hands shook when I finally pulled the key from my purse. I only had one glass of wine, so I couldn't blame alcohol for my inability to concentrate. I could place the blame squarely on Archer, his too dark eyes, his too smooth smile, and his spicy-citrus scent.

"Let me help you with that." He snatched the key from my grasp before I could object.

I watched as he pushed my front door open. Even the familiar squeak of the hinges didn't interrupt the charged air buzzing between us. Transfixed, ten seconds crawled like an hour as I stood, waiting for something. That's when it hit me like a firm slap across the face. *I wanted him to kiss me*. Where the hell did that come from?

His eyes dropped to my mouth, and my lips

tingled, craving the moment he made contact. *Oh shit. He wanted to kiss me too.*

No.

No.

No.

I promised myself I wouldn't go down this road again—that I'd stay light-years away from anyone affiliated with my stepdad—but less than an hour in Archer's company and I wanted to make an exception.

"Well, goodnight," I said, turning my head to the side, severing the connection shimmering between us, willing it to disappear entirely both physically and mentally. My muscles still strung tight with anticipation and longing, I played with the metal latch on my clutch, opening and closing it.

Click.

Click.

Click.

"Goodnight," he responded.

If I had kept my eyes on his instead of staring at the scuff on the tip of my right heel, I would've predicted his next move and sidestepped it, but I didn't. I was too busy processing what had almost happened and clicking the latch of my clutch to consider what could happen.

Quick as lightning and without giving me the opportunity to evade him, he cupped my face and pressed his lips warmly against mine, back and forth. Blood roared in my ears like a freight train, growing louder and louder with each brush of his firm lips. He tasted like bourbon, and he smelled like a spicy slice of heaven. The energy sizzled between us like nothing I'd ever experienced before. I molded my body against his, forgetting who he was, who I was. None of that mattered.

But within a flash, he stepped back. The kiss had ended before it started. Irrationally disappointed, my eyes sought out his, and the cocky bastard grinned, probably because I gave in. "I'll pick you up on Sunday for lunch. Be ready at noon."

He spun around and jogged down the stairs, never looking back. I guess he didn't want to give me a chance to snub his invitation. I wouldn't have rejected him, not after that kiss. I already bought what he was selling, but he didn't need to know that.

I closed the door and leaned against it, my body sagging with relief and longing. I felt like I had spent the last five minutes in a lightning storm, dodging fate. My heart battered the walls of my chest, and my muscles felt like an elastic exercise band stretched tight and ready to snap. One simple brush of his lips and I was like a powder keg of desire, ready to explode with even the slightest spark.

Sunday. The day after tomorrow. I had a date. Six months had elapsed since my last one. Hopefully this one would end better than that one. If my reaction to his kiss was any indication, it would, and that fact scared me.

CHAPTER FIVE

Langley

"Thomas would like a moment of your time in his office before we leave." My mom opened the door to the home she had shared with my stepdad for the last ten years.

Though petite, only five foot three and one hundred pounds, she was a force of her own. She landed a world-renowned actor in her twenties and a distinguished senator in her thirties, and over the years, more than one person had been reduced to tears by the strength of her icy words and frozen glare.

I tapped the strings of my covered tennis racket against my leg and then twirled it between my hands. Today was our weekly tennis match.

Saying my mom and I didn't have anything in common was an understatement. For starters, tennis wasn't my thing, but she loved it. Don't get me wrong. I loved to exercise. Five days a week, I exercised every morning at the physical therapy office where I worked, but I hated tennis. My mom forced me to play as a child, which probably explained some of my distaste for the sport. She knew that, but for some reason she deemed it the perfect once a week mother-daughter activity, which suited me. Running back and forth while slamming a ball over the net made it difficult to have a meaningful conversation—something I avoided at all costs.

"I don't have time today. I have to catch up on some paperwork at the office." I cringed inwardly at the lie. I never worked on the weekends. We both knew it.

"He's your dad. Show some respect."

"Stepdad," I corrected without any heat. This argument was so old, the lines so familiar that I should've taped our first conversation a decade ago and played it every time she brought up the subject. It would've saved us both a lot of time.

"He considers you his daughter. He offered to make it official, but you refused."

I rolled my eyes. "Because I had a dad. I don't need another one." I had eavesdropped often enough to know that my stepdad only agreed to adopt me because my mom demanded it, and even then, he didn't relent until three months before my eighteenth birthday. Besides, I wasn't blind. He didn't feel any fatherly affection for me, or at least nothing he expressed outwardly.

"He didn't raise you...not like your stepdad."

"Senator Wharton doesn't have anything to do with the person I've become." Just the thought of giving my stepdad credit for anything in my life made my chest ache with emptiness. Sure, the first year after they married, he showed up at my sports events and attended parent-teacher conferences, but by the time I graduated from high school, he stopped making any effort. He didn't even attend my high school or college graduation.

My mom's lips thinned and she dropped her chin, disguising her reaction, but I didn't need to see it to sense her disappointment. It vibrated around us in heavy waves, beating at my chest, squeezing my ribcage until I couldn't breathe. My mom didn't trade barbs or yell. That would be beneath her. Silent, thick, guilt was her weapon of choice, and she wielded it like a knife, slicing away little pieces of her target until she got what she wanted. "I'm sorry we failed to meet your expectations as parents."

I glanced at my watch to indicate my impatience. "Is he ready to see me?" I asked, ignoring her comment. I refused to take her bait.

She pushed her dark hair away from her face with two expertly manicured fingers. "I think so, but knock before you go in."

Without another word, I wove through the stark white paneled hallway, treading with feather soft steps over the black and white checkered marble floor. Traditional black mullioned windows lined one side of the hallway, and polished nickel lanterns hung at even intervals from the barrel-vaulted ceiling.

At the end of the hall, I came face to face with espresso-stained double wood doors marking the entry into Senator Thomas Wharton's private domain. I banged my knuckles against the heavy door twice, and then I lowered my hand to my side, curling the fingers around the hem of my black and gray tennis skirt. The sound bounced unnaturally off the walls. God, I hated this house. It reminded me of a museum rather than a home.

"Come in," he said.

I cracked the door, eased my eyes around the corner, and peeked inside before crossing the threshold. Light and bright colorless walls ceded control to dark, heavy wood-paneled walls. A plush, diamond patterned sapphire-blue and saffron-colored rug covered all but the one foot perimeter of the dark hardwood floor. Two burgundy leather chairs sat in front of his oversized desk. Dark wood floor-to-ceiling shelves held thousands of leather bound books.

My stepdad never wanted a private audience with me in his study unless he intended to chastise my behavior, and as I crossed the room, dread seeped into chest. My hands were clammy, and my heart fluttered against my breastbone like a caged butterfly. Even at the age of twenty-four, I still had a hard time seeing him as a normal man who I could discuss things with on equal footing. I didn't want him to hold this invisible power over me anymore. I needed to take control of my life, but it was easier said than done.

I ran fingers over the brass nail heads on the top of the burgundy leather chairs, silently counting each one of them. Counting calmed me.

One.

Two.

Three.

Four…

When I counted the last one on the back of the chair, I squared my shoulders and took a seat.

"My mom said you wanted to talk to me." I crossed my ankles to stifle the budding urge to bounce my knee up and down like a child being reprimanded for bad behavior.

Senator Wharton leaned back in his chair. He was a tall, thin man with a head of dark hair that had begun to gray at the temples in the last two years. His eyes were dark and unreadable as usual. He was a politician, after all. Wasn't that a prerequisite?

"You didn't stay long last night." It was a statement, not a question.

I dropped my eyes to my lap. "Two hours." After all these years, the man still managed to intimidate me with a few words or a well-placed glare.

He fingered the edge of a stack of papers and newspaper articles on his desk. Unlike most people who read their news online, Senator Wharton still had his staff assemble a daily briefing summarizing the news they thought worthy of his attention.

He cocked his head to the side and steepled his fingers in front of his chest like a man accustomed to getting his way, and Senator Wharton was accustomed to getting his way on and off the senate floor. "Did you talk to anyone new?"

Sensing the trap closing in around me, my eyes flitted around the room before landing once again on Senator Wharton. "Well, I…" I cleared my throat, composing my thoughts. Clearly, he wanted to discuss Archer, but I didn't understand why or how he got wind of our encounter. I decided to offer a vague answer until I understood his angle. "I met a few new people."

Senator Wharton rested his elbows on the edge of his desk, and his lips thinned into firm, hard lines. Just like that, the battle lines were drawn. "Hm...interesting. I thought you were acquainted with just about everyone there. I'll have to be more diligent about introducing you to everyone next time. With the official launch of my presidency in two weeks, you to need study the talking points and memorize faces and names."

Two weeks. That was news to me. I took a deep breath. "Sure. That's probably a good idea," I said, even though I would rather stick a hot poker in my eye than contribute time to his campaign.

He took a sip of the amber liquid in diamond patterned cut crystal glass. "What about Archer Black? Was he one of the people you met?"

Like a finger tracing the individual bumps of my spine, a slow shiver traveled through me. "I think so," I answered, my voice as detached as I could make it.

"How long have you known him?" Tension creased his forehead into thick ribbons.

"We already covered this. He's one of the people I met last night."

Senator Wharton slid a newspaper article across his desk. "Can you explain this?"

I kept my eyes locked on his. We were like two dueling adversaries awaiting the signal to fire at will. I wanted him to know I wouldn't meekly bend to his will.

After an exhaustive beat, he nodded his head and I canted forward, slowly lowering my gaze to the article. A picture of Archer and me leaving the fundraiser last night covered the top quarter of the paper. His hand cradled my lower back as we gazed fondly at each other. The image painted a picture of intimacy that hadn't existed in real life, or at least not at that moment. When he dropped me off at my house later that night, it was a different story. At least the photographers didn't make the effort to follow me home.

I shrugged and leaned back in the chair. "We shared a taxi to The Lux. He met his date, and I met Winnie."

His eyes narrowed and he pushed his chair back. "That's it? There's nothing else you want to add?"

"That's it."

"And you don't have plans to see him again?"

My eyes darted to the side, taking in the scenic flowers outside the bay window of his office. I rubbed my arms as though I were cold. "I don't get why you're interested in Archer Black or my connection to him."

Senator Wharton drummed his fingers on the table, the cadence echoing unnaturally through the room. "Archer Black has a rather unsavory reputation. I don't want you to associate with him, especially during my campaign."

My back tensed and my hands white-knuckled the arms of the chair as a sudden burst of anger surged through me. "I'm well past the age when you can tell me who I can and can't talk to. Besides, he's not so unsavory that you'd refuse to take his money. Wasn't that why you invited him to your fundraiser?"

"I'm not taking his money."

"Because he didn't offer it."

Senator Wharton sighed. "You're associated with me, and anything you do affects my image. This is an important year for me. As I said, I'm going to announce my intention to run for president in two weeks or so."

I popped out of my chair like a jack in the box. "And anything you do affects me, but I haven't forced you to stop."

"What's that supposed to mean?"

Uncomfortable silence stretched between us, the tension in the room so weighty I thought my knees would buckle under his glare. "I don't know. Nothing." I couldn't tell him anything. I made my decision six months ago. I couldn't change course now.

"Fine." He folded the newspaper article into fourths. "Your mother is probably waiting for you."

I stood up and walked toward the door without another word. How old did I have to be before Senator Wharton stopped trying to control me?

As my hand circled the polished nickel door lever, Senator Wharton dropped his hand on my shoulder. He flashed a phony smile, complete with his signature dimple. "Please stay away from Archer Black. I don't want you to get hurt. Even though I never adopted you, you're still like a daughter to me. I love you, Langley. I only want what's best for you and our family, and Archer

Black is not it."

I stepped out of his grasp. "Thanks for your concern," I answered instead of promising anything. I hated empty promises and half-truths. I would play along for the sake of his campaign, but I wouldn't let my stepdad dictate my personal relationships. I had every intention of seeing Archer again. Since he had left me on my doorstep Friday night, his dark hair and even darker eyes kept drifting to the forefront of my mind. My stomach fluttered like it was filled with Pop Rocks every time I thought of him. I hadn't been really interested in or tempted by a man in a long time. For that reason alone, I wanted to see him one more time, even if he was a complication I couldn't afford right now.

CHAPTER SIX

Archer

At exactly twelve in the afternoon on Sunday, I knocked on Langley's door with a bouquet of her favorite flowers—pink peonies—in hand. I planned to take her to her favorite restaurant for her favorite food. Without asking, I knew all this and more about Langley.

The last three months of my life, I had poured over the details of her life, committing every preference and detail to memory. I knew where she lived long before I escorted her home two days ago. Senator Wharton owned her townhome and rented it to her for twenty percent below market value. She worked as a physical therapist, but she always wanted to pursue an acting career and follow in her dad's footsteps. Unbeknownst to Langley, her mom sabotaged her chosen profession by turning down roles and casting calls without her consent.

Red was her favorite color. She dated Brandon for six months. She had four serious boyfriends since she turned eighteen. Her mother introduced her to each and every one of those men, except one. When she turned thirty, she would gain control of the trust created by her deceased father. Her mother had skimmed around a million dollars from Langley's trust in the two years before she married Senator Wharton.

I had a whole file cabinet filled with miscellaneous details about Langley's life. Nothing was too small. After all, I needed every piece of information I could get to accomplish my goal, but I overlooked one thing. A big fucking wildcard in the dangerous game I started last night—we had chemistry. Too much chemistry. There were hundreds of reasons why I shouldn't be interested in Langley, but the minute I met her, none of them mattered. If I were smart, I'd ignore the tension crackling like lightning between us, but I couldn't. It was too overpowering.

"Hi," Langley said when she flung open the door less than a minute later. She wore black slim-fitting pants and a creamy sweater that highlighted her sun-kissed hair, making it look like a halo.

"Hi." I held out the bouquet of flowers.

"I love peonies," she said, taking them out of my hand and holding them to her nose. "Did someone tell you?"

"Just a lucky guess," I lied.

"Come in." She waved me into her townhome.

"This place is nice." I took in the large windows, the newly refinished hardwood floors, and the gleaming white kitchen cabinets.

"Thanks. I couldn't afford it if my stepdad didn't

lower the rent, but I'm going to buy it from him in a couple months if he agrees."

"I didn't think a physical therapist made that much money." The purchase price of a townhome like this in Georgetown easily exceeded one million dollars. I'm sure she planned to buy it with the funds from her trust, but I wasn't supposed to know anything about it. Not many people did.

She filled a white bone china vase with water. "How did you know I'm a physical therapist? I don't remember mentioning it."

"I did my research."

Her brows furrowed. "You Googled me?"

"Didn't you Google me?" I said, deflecting her question because I did a whole lot more than Google her. I investigated every part of her life I could feasibly get my hands on. Her school records. Her family history. Her medical history. Her friends. Nothing was too small.

A smile danced on her lips as she fiddled with the flowers. "I might have."

"And what did you decide?"

I wasn't worried. I kept a tight leash on the details of my private life. Only information I approved and leaked to the press could be found in an internet search, and I never dated without signing a nondisclosure agreement. I preferred it that way. Other than the carefully crafted narrative of my childhood and pictures of me at benefit dinners with dates, not much information was available.

"That you either have a great publicist who controls your information with an iron fist or that you live a relatively uneventful life."

I chuckled. "Both are true. I don't like my private affairs spilled on the pages of magazines or internet websites. A clean image is imperative when you own a large financial firm that manages billions of dollars." All of that was true, but I also had a dirty, soul-shattering childhood I wanted to keep private.

"Then you probably didn't appreciate the picture of us that made it into the Saturday morning paper."

"I didn't mind." The photographs were there because I wanted them there. I wanted Senator Wharton to see us together. It was just the beginning of what I had planned to draw Senator Wharton out of his comfort zone.

She rubbed her hands along the sides of her pants. "I can't say I agree."

"What do you mean?"

"My stepdad made it clear he didn't want me involved with you."

Perfect. I raised one eyebrow. "Is that your way of canceling our date?"

"No," she said quickly, raising her hands in front of her, and then she laughed, a slightly rusty sound that pierced straight through my heart. "I think I'm old enough to decide who I want in my life."

"Then we're still on for lunch?"

"As long as you're not offended by the fact my stepdad disapproves of you." Her cat-like greenish eyes were still strained, but she seemed less guarded than when she answered the door five minutes ago.

I paused, hands buried in my pockets. Then, I moved forward, wrapping my arms around her waist and pinning her against her kitchen counter.

Her muscles tightened under my fingertips, but within seconds she relaxed, her body melting against mine.

When she lifted her head, I didn't waste any time. My lips covered hers. She didn't push me away. Not even close. She let out a soft moan, but I didn't want to spook her, so I continued kissing her softly without rushing this thing between us. My tongue slid slowly around hers, testing her reaction, evaluating every welcoming stroke and delicious curl.

Her heart hammered against my chest, and my body vibrated with desire. Her kiss tasted better than I had imagined, not that I'd spent much time thinking about kissing her since Friday night. No, that's a lie. The minute I met her in person two nights ago, I wanted to kiss her and a whole lot more. But fuck, I needed to temper my reaction to her. Langley and I had a pre-determined expiration date, one that would be accompanied by fireworks of the disastrous sort.

I stepped back, needing space, needing walls between us, because walls were all there ever could be. "Are you ready to go?"

Langley sucked in a breath, her eyes studying me, searching me, but she wouldn't see anything except the charming veneer I showed everyone. I mastered the look before my tenth birthday.

No one knew me the real me, except Knox and my mom, and she died six months ago in an apparent suicide. A neighbor found her dead on the floor of our dirty trailer, a gun in one hand and half her head missing.

My family lived waist-deep in the same dirty secrets in the same dirty world. They'd been woven into the fabric of our very existence, coloring every choice and every relationship, new and old. My mom promised Senator Wharton she'd keep those secrets, and she did. She took them to her grave, but she made those promises, not me. Once she died, I considered her debts satisfied. Now, I could do whatever I wanted with the information.

"Where are we going?" she asked, running her fingertip over her swollen lips.

"The Edge."

"Ugh," she groaned. "I hate that place."

"What?" My eyebrows snapped together.

"No." She laughed. "But you must be a mind reader, or the information you found about me online was far more revealing than I'd like. First the peonies and now The Edge."

"I aim to please."

"Well, I hate to admit it, but you're doing a good job so far."

I threaded my fingers through hers. Damn, this might be easier than I'd thought.

***

She stared forlornly at her nearly empty dessert plate, only a swirl of chocolate and raspberry sauce remained. Unquestionably, The Edge was Langley's favorite restaurant.

"Do you want anything else?" I asked. "Are you still hungry?"

She laughed. "You're making fun of me."

"No." I shook my head. "I'm glad you enjoyed your meal."

She placed her silverware diagonally across her plate and pushed it to the center of the table. "Ugh. I'm so full. I feel like I'm going to explode. I'll have to exercise twice as long tomorrow morning to make up for this lunch."

"Do you exercise every day?"

"I'm a physical therapist," she answered, as though that's all she needed to say.

"So?" I prompted, prying her for more information even though both my reports and her long, lean muscles already answered my question.

"I work in a gym of sorts, so I end up doing some exercise every day at work, and my mom and I have a standing tennis date on Saturday mornings."

"Are you and your mom close?" My research suggested they weren't, but that might not be Langley's perception of their relationship.

She chewed on her lip, clearly contemplating her answer. "Growing up, my dad was larger than life. I idolized him. For the first ten years of my life, I was his shadow. When he died, it was just my mom and me for a couple of years. I love her. She's my mom, but we never really clicked. I don't understand her, and she doesn't understand me. What about your mom?"

"She was a single mom, so she wasn't around a lot. It always seemed like it was my brother Knox and me against the world. We did everything together."

She nodded. "You're lucky. I wish I had a

brother or a sister. When my mom remarried, I thought my stepdad would want kids, but it never happened. He focused on his career and my mom focused on reinventing herself. There wasn't much room left for anything else."

"Reinventing herself?" I asked, ignoring the topic of Senator Wharton and kids entirely.

"When she married Senator Wharton, she transformed from Hollywood wife to the doting wife of a politician. She replaced her flashy clothes with simple lined dresses and pantsuits. She spent her days volunteering for causes I don't think she knew existed before her second marriage." She frowned and shook her head.

"Did that trouble you?"

"It shouldn't have, but at the time I felt like she wanted to erase the memory of my dad and the first ten years of our lives."

I slanted forward, bracing my elbows on the edge of the table. "Now what do you think?"

"Maybe it was her way of dealing with the grief. For the most part, I went along with what she wanted, but I refused to let Senator Wharton adopt me."

"Why?"

She twisted her hands in her lap. "Because I had a dad. I didn't need another one. Besides, he was barely around, so it felt forced. I don't think he really wanted to adopt me. Contrary to what is reported in the media, we're not close," she confessed.

I nodded, not saying anything for a few prolonged seconds. Truth be told, I was shocked.

My files were littered with articles of how Senator Wharton embraced his role of parent to Langley. "I didn't realize."

"Nobody knows that, except for Winnie." She laughed. "She's the keeper of all my secrets. I don't know what I'd do without her."

"I'll have to keep that in mind," I answered with a grin.

"You'll never get anything out of her. We took a blood covenant as kids. I've sworn her to secrecy."

I raised my eyebrows. "Now I'm really curious about all these secrets that necessitate a blood covenant."

"They're serious." She nodded, her eyes wide in mock innocence.

I winked. "Can you give me a hint?"

She gazed at her lap for a second and then exhaled loudly. "Okay, but you have to promise never to tell."

I held up one hand. "I promise."

"I cheated on my fifth grade spelling test. I wrote a word along the inside of my index finger."

"What word?"

"Ubiquitous," she whispered.

I burst out laughing. "With secrets like those, you definitely need a blood covenant."

"Now that I've told you my darkest secret, you have to tell me one. An eye for an eye."

"Eye for an eye?" I mocked, purposely changing the direction of the conversation. Unlike Langley, I had too many dark secrets.

"As long as we're on the theme of blood covenants, I thought I'd throw in some more biblical references." She shrugged. "Now stop procrastinating and share something."

"Something?"

She rolled her eyes. "Anything."

"Fine." I tapped my fingers on the table as I considered my options. Notably, my thoughts kept circling back to the one secret I couldn't share. Was that an indication of a guilty conscience? Because as I stared into her glowing green eyes and soaked in her supple smile, I felt a twinge of discomfort ripple down my spine.

When I decided to pull Langley into my plans, she was just a name on a piece of paper. With each passing second I spent with her, she showed me she was so much more. She was quickly getting under my skin, which wasn't a good thing. I needed to figure out a way for her to trust me while keeping her at an arm's length.

"Knox and I used to pocket money from the fountain at the mall," I finally revealed.

"Hey." She smacked my hand lightly. "You stole people's dreams for the future."

My gut twisted. Things hadn't changed much.

"We didn't have a choice. We needed to eat." I chuckled, angling to lighten the moment.

Sadness flashed across her face, further entrenching the remorse and guilt simmering inside of me. "Then, you're forgiven."

I smiled faintly. If only she'd offer those same words when I finished destroying Senator Wharton.

CHAPTER SEVEN

Langley

"Just one more set of ten. You're almost done." I loved helping my patients get their life back, and Mr. Wright wasn't an exception. Three months ago, he fell off a ladder cleaning the leaves out of his gutters. Two bulging discs that pressed on his root nerve made him a candidate for surgery, or at the very least, shots. He decided to try physical therapy first. Now, he was back at work and almost as good as new. He probably had one or two weeks left before I would release him from my care.

"You're a slave driver," Mr. Wright said as he started another set of sit-ups on the silver exercise ball.

"You need to improve your core strength to support your lower back," I said, adjusting the angle of his head to minimize any neck strain.

I counted down his final reps. "Seven. Eight. Nine. Ten, and you're done."

"Thank God," Mr. Wright said, rolling off the

ball onto his back before standing up. "How much longer until I'm done with rehab?"

I shook my finger at him. "One week. Maybe two, but that doesn't mean you can stop doing your exercises, or you'll end up back here or in surgery."

He groaned as he lifted his gym bag. "I know. I'll see you on Friday."

I barely had time to finish my paperwork before Winnie peeked inside the front door of my office. "Hey," she said, lifting her hand in greeting. "Are you ready for lunch?"

"Yes, but I only have forty-five minutes before my next appointment, so it has to be quick."

Winnie held up a white paper bag. "I figured as much. You're always overscheduled, but never fear, I brought take out."

"Did I ever tell you that you're amazing?"

"No, but don't let that stop you from singing my praises now." Winnie dropped the bag of food on the desk and plopped down on the small black side chair. My office wasn't impressive. It barely qualified as an office. It was more of a glorified cubicle with a door.

"So what's for lunch?" I unrolled the top of the bag and peeked inside.

"Kale salads and cold-pressed juice, but there's a surprise at the bottom, so wipe that frown off your face."

"Magic bars," I held up the bag of cookies and dangled it in front of me. "I love you."

"I know. Most people do." She laughed at her joke as I placed the salads and green mystery drink in front of us.

"You're not working today?" I asked as I poured the dressing on top of my salad.

"Not really. I went in for a couple hours, but they sent me home."

Winnie was a paralegal. Normally, she worked at least sixty hours a week, but everything came to a grinding halt three weeks ago. The partner she worked for had an emergency surgery and he hadn't returned to the office yet. The other attorneys had given her a few small projects the first week, but now she didn't have anything to do except make a few phone calls every day.

"Any word on Mr. Brandt?"

She shook her head. "Nothing, which makes me think it's really bad. If I don't hear anything by the end of this week, I'm going to start looking for another job."

"That's probably a good idea." I took a sip of the green juice, and my sour taste buds went on high alert, flooding my mouth with saliva. "What the hell is in here?"

Winnie smirked. "Lots of lemon mixed with spinach, avocado, and a dash of pineapple juice."

"Don't buy it again."

"It's supposed to lift your energy and wake you up."

"Wake up your taste buds, you mean."

She took a sip of her juice. "Yeah, I see what you mean. It's a definite no repeat item."

"It even sounds terrible. Why did you pick it?" I took one more drink and tossed it in the trash.

"The guy at the counter recommended it." She bit her lip and turned to the side. "He was cute and I didn't want to hurt his feelings."

"So you decided to hurt us instead."

She laughed. "I guess so."

"Stick to the basics next time."

Winnie tapped her fork on the side of the black plastic salad container. "I saw the picture of you with Archer Black in the paper."

"Yeah, so did my stepdad. He summoned me to his office the next day to discuss it. He warned me to stay away from him."

Winnie rolled her eyes. "Why didn't you tell me the picture you texted me was of him?"

"I didn't know at the time."

"How could you not know?"

I leaned back in my chair. "We shared a taxi. He introduced himself as Archer. I didn't ask any other questions."

"You do know he's possibly the most eligible bachelor on the east coast, right?"

"I might have read something about that."

"You should cyberstalk him to figure out how to accidently run into him again, and this time you need to get his phone number and at least one date."

I stuffed a pile of kale into my mouth to prevent me having to reply right away. Four days had passed since Archer took me out to lunch.

"I have his phone number, and we did go on a date last Sunday. We had a great time. He gave me peonies—my all-time favorite flower. We ate at my all-time favorite restaurant. The conversation never lulled. His goodnight kiss was perfect in a 'make my knees weak and my lips tingle kind of way.'"

"What?" Winnie slammed her hands on the top

of my desk. "And you never said a word? What kind of friend are you?"

I fiddled with the paper napkin in my lap, twisting it until it resembled a feminine hygiene product. I totally misread our date. I would've bet half my trust fund that a second date lurked on the not too distant horizon. Now that four days had passed without a single word, I wouldn't bet one dollar. Apparently, he succeeded at impressing me, but I didn't do the same.

I sighed. "The first couple of days after the date, I was slammed with patients. Now it's irrelevant. He hasn't·called me. I don't think he's interested."

"You don't know that. He could be out of town. He could have crazy things happening at work. Four days is nothing." She waved her hand in front of her face to emphasize the point.

"Okay, so how many days before I write him off?"

Winnie corkscrewed her finger in her hair over and over, and then released it and started the process over again. She'd done this since we were kids when she was thinking or stalling. It was a miracle she still had any hair on the right side of her head. "A week."

My eyebrows scaled my forehead. "A week," I echoed. "And what if he calls after a week? What does that mean?"

"It means he's not really that interested, or that he's a wannabe player or a flat-out jerk. Either way, on the eighth day, your wait is over. If he calls after that, you don't want to talk to him anyway, and if he doesn't call, you move on. Erase his number and scrub him from your memory."

"So I have four more days of waiting." I sagged in my chair. "That sucks. I thought the date went really well. I don't get it."

"I know. Dating sucks. When we were kids, I thought we'd both be married or in a serious relationship by the time we hit twenty-five."

"Hey," I said, holding up my hand, "you may be twenty-five, but I still have three more months of my early twenties, and I intend to live every one of them without fast-forwarding through the last ninety days."

Winnie pointed at the dry erase board calendar on my wall. "It's actually more like eighty-five days."

My eyes narrowed, but the corners of my lips twitched. "You suck."

"Wait." She giggled. "You told me I was amazing twenty minutes ago. You're giving me whiplash."

"Yeah, well, now I'm retracting my compliment."

Winnie gathered up her salad and plastic utensils and stuffed them into the white paper bag. "No you're not."

"You're right. I love you."

"Right back at you," she said, brushing invisible crumbs from her lap. Winnie wasn't the touchy-feely sort, but I meant it. I did love her. She'd been my best friend since the first day I started middle school in D.C. My mom had yanked me out of my school in L.A. a week after my dad died of a drug overdose and moved us across the country. She grew up in Potomac, Maryland, so my mom figured I should too. According to her, there was no reason to stay in L.A. after my dad died.

Going from L.A. to Maryland at the age of ten, I had experienced an immediate and heavy dose of culture shock. I don't think I would have remained sane through all the changes in my life without Winnie as a best friend. I was permanently indebted to her for befriending me and so many other things she'd done for me over the years.

"Do you want to go out for drinks after work on Friday?" she asked as she opened my office door.

"Sure. Text me the place and the time."

CHAPTER EIGHT

Archer

"Do you have plans tonight?"

Deafening silence hummed through the phone. If I concentrated hard enough, I could hear the sound of the wireless radio waves rippling through my phone. Five, almost six, days had passed since I made contact with Langley. At least ten times during the week I picked up my phone after mentally composing a text or scripting the beginning of a phone conversation, but I never pulled the trigger, which was a bad move judging by Langley's lack of an immediate response.

"It's Friday night," she finally answered, as though those simple words said everything, and they did, or at least for most of the single population.

"I know what day it is."

"And that means I have plans."

"What kind of plans?" I planted my feet on top of the smooth walnut surface of my desk. It had been a shitty week. Meeting after meeting with new and existing clients kept me from doing anything except work, which was great for the future of Black Investments, but not so great for developing a relationship with Langley, and I needed to get her on my side, at least temporarily.

"I'm going out for drinks."

"Can I join you? We can go to dinner after."

Papers rustled in the background. "I don't know. Maybe some other time would be better."

Nope. This wouldn't work. I fucked up this week, but I didn't have time to be shoved off for another week due to my utter stupidity. Everything had to be perfectly timed for my plan to succeed. "Look, Langley. I'm sorry I didn't call or text earlier. I never intended to blow you off for five days."

"Then why did you? On Sunday, you said you wanted to meet for lunch this week. Well, this week is pretty much over."

Squeezing my phone harder than necessary, I blew out an exaggerated breath. "Work. It's been a strange week. I had appointments with new clients every day and I couldn't—"

"So many appointments that you couldn't spare twenty seconds to send a one sentence text?" She scoffed. "Oh please. I'm not eighteen. I can read between the lines. You're not that interested."

"No, you're wrong. I'm definitely interested. I made a mistake. It won't happen again."

"You're right. It won't, because I'm not big on second chances anymore. They're a waste of energy at the beginning of a relationship. If it starts bad, it ends bad. No need to experience all the torture in the middle."

"Is that your motto?" I slid my feet from the desk and stood up.

"No, but it's a good one. I think I'll adopt it and put it into action starting with you."

"Langley, I'm sorry."

"Look, I'm running late. Maybe we can talk in...oh...." She paused as though she were evaluating her calendar. "Five more days. I'll call you if I'm not too busy at work. How's that sound?"

Fuck. Total miscalculation on my part. Shocked by how much I enjoyed our date, I wanted to put some space between us. It was fine if she fell for me, but I didn't have that luxury. "Wait. Don't hang up."

"I'm busy. You didn't have time to talk this week, and I don't have time to talk right now."

"Give me five minutes."

"Why? You couldn't give me twenty seconds all week."

"Tell me where you're going. I'll meet you there. I'll make it up to you."

"Sorry. I don't have time. People are waiting for me, and I don't like to make people wait unnecessarily."

"Just give me the name of the bar."

"No."

"How about the address or latitude and longitude?"

"No. Not happening. I'm meeting someone. I don't want you there."

"A date?"

"Yes."

"Like with another guy?" I picked up my jacket and tossed it over my arm. Langley hadn't dated anyone since Brandon, so it didn't seem likely, but what did I know?

"No."

"Okay, then give me a clue, and if I'm able to decipher it, you'll give me a second chance. If not, then this ends here and now. I won't bug you again. You can embrace your new motto and move on to the next guy."

"Are you serious?"

"Dead serious," I responded without even second-guessing it. I'd use every last resource in my arsenal to track her down. I didn't have an alternative. Sure, I could have copious amounts of peonies delivered to her house all weekend, but I needed to see her in order to move things forward.

"Hm. I don't know. Let me think about this."

"You won't regret it. I promise."

"How do you figure?"

"If I track you down, I'll buy your drinks and your dinner."

"That's a given. I need a better incentive."

And there it was. I heard the smile in her voice loud and clear. She was going to cave. I pumped my fist in the air. Adolescent, I know, but I'd been waiting my whole life to get revenge. "I'll buy drinks and dinner for you and your friends."

"No matter how many. You're not going to limit the number of friends, right?"

Fuck. I didn't care. I'd buy dinner for thirty people, no, a hundred. "Within reason."

"Fine. I'll give you a clue, but if you fail to show up, don't bother calling me again."

"Agreed, I'll delete your phone number, except I have to insist on an Act of God clause."

"An act of God—what in the hell are you talking about?"

I chuckled. "You know, the clause in every contract that excuses performance for things or events outside the control of either party."

"Like what?"

I pressed the button to call the elevator. I needed as much time as possible to figure out her clue. "You know…earthquake, hurricane, tornado, terrorist attack."

"Got it. I think we're safe on that front."

"You never know."

"Okay, then barring an act of God, you have until nine to find me. Good luck."

The elevator opened, and I stepped inside. I prayed my phone had a strong signal, and it didn't drop the call before I got the clue. "Wait. I need the clue."

She chuckled. "Get with the game. I already gave it to you. See you at nine."

"What?"

"That's right. Figure it out."

The line went dead, whether from the elevator or Langley disconnecting the call, I didn't know. Shit. I had less than four hours and counting to find her. I should've taped our conversation so I could replay every word. Now I only had my memory to rely on, and I'd been preoccupied trying to get the hell out of the office and start my search.

I replayed the highlights of our conversation and cross-referenced it with bars in the city.

Mottos.

Second Chances.

Dinner.

Friends.

Acts of God.

Nine.

I chuckled as I opened the passenger door of my car service. Well played, Langley.

CHAPTER NINE

Langley

"You know I really hate this place. Why'd you change our plans at the last second?" Winnie asked as we elbowed our way through the wall of people to get a drink. Finding a table or a chair would be unlikely.

"Long story," I said, groaning as someone's drink splashed on my arm.

"If you're going to subject me to this scene when we planned to have a drink at the restaurant bar before we ate dinner, you need to offer an explanation." She glared at me over her shoulder. "I'm starving by the way, and there is no way in hell I'm going to touch the toxic pretzel, nut combination." She visibly shivered.

"Fine." We managed to snag two stools at the bar. I draped my purse over my lap. "We're meeting Archer here."

Her eyebrows scaled her forehead. "And he picked this bar."

"No. I picked it."

"Seriously?"

"He called me as I was leaving the office. He wanted to meet."

"So, you immediately decided that because I hate The Nine Bar, he should meet us here."

"Not exactly. I told him I had plans, and I'd call him in five days or not." Actually, at the time, part of me wanted nothing more than to meet him for a drink and dinner. But the other part of me—the part that didn't have any problem ignoring his velvety, smooth voice and the memory of his lips against mine—pleaded with me to avoid leaping into a romantic entanglement with Archer. My relationship with Brandon took a sickening turn after six months of envisioning a future with him, and no matter how nebulous, I didn't like Archer's connection to my stepdad.

"Oh." Winnie slapped me on the arm. "That's good."

I smiled. "I thought so, but he wouldn't let it go, and before I knew it, I had promised him a hint of where we planned to go. If he found us, I'd give him a second chance. If not, then he promised to delete my number." With my index finger, I spun the rectangular coaster on the counter in circles until the beer label resembled a cardboard kaleidoscope. "The Nine Bar was the first thing that popped into my head."

"So here we are."

"Yep, that's about it."

"You know what I think?" she asked, her light blue eyes twinkling.

I rolled my eyes. "Do I want to know?"

"Whatever." She waved her hand in front of her. "If he likes this lame ass bar, you should dump him on the spot. Don't even offer an explanation. I mean, look at the guys that frequent this place."

Casually, I glanced to the side, down the length of the bar. Slicked back hair, jeans tighter than my tightest pair, thighs smaller than mine, and skintight shirts were just a few glaring things that had my gag reflex on high alert. Call me a throwback to fifties, but I liked real men—muscles and testosterone included—not men that shared my jean size and cried at chick flicks. "I see what you mean."

"White wine?" she asked when the bartender paused in front of us, his hands on his hips.

"No. I need something stronger. Grey Goose on the rocks with a twist of lime."

"Make it two," Winnie said, and then she swiveled on her stool to face me. "So are you nervous to see Archer?"

I rubbed my hands up and down my thighs. "A little. I had written him off and then he called. I don't know what to expect."

"Don't expect anything. It's better for the ego."

"I'll keep that in mind," I said as I lifted the lowball glass to my lips.

Not two minutes later, two warm hands landed on my shoulders.

"I didn't know if you really meant for me to meet you at nine at The Nine Bar. If so, I'm a couple hours early."

"Archer," I said, glancing at him over my shoulder. Like the night I met him, his six foot two body was dressed in a dark, custom fit suit that emphasized his lean muscled body. My heart ricocheted off the walls of my chest, and my stomach freefell through my adnominal cavity. I willed my body to remain unaffected and calm, but the winged creatures in my stomach refused to be tamed. This man did crazy things to me.

"Langley," he responded, his heated dark stare melting me in a pile of mush. He held my eyes for a moment. Electricity ping-ponged in the air around us, buzzing like cicadas in late summer. *Kiss me,* my stupid, love-struck alter ego silently begged. His lips curved into a half smile, and any lingering reservations about Archer sunk faster than the Titanic.

Like a moon succumbing to the gravitational pull of a planet, my body tilted toward his. My eyes fluttered. My lips tingled, imagining the moment of impact.

Closer.

Closer.

So close, I saw the gold specks in his irises.

Then, bam…Winnie cleared her throat. I shook my head, dislodging the Archer-induced fog filling my brain.

"Winnie, this is Archer," I said, blood rushing to my face. Thank God the bar was dimly lit.

"Nice to meet you." Archer shook her hand.

"Just one friend?" Archer asked, refocusing his mind-wilting attention on me.

"I thought I'd go easy on you." I shrugged. "Besides, I didn't want to promise an army of friends free drinks and dinner if you didn't show."

"I told you I'd find you." He squeezed my shoulders and then dropped his hands to his sides.

"You did, but you also said we'd go to lunch this week." I should have let the topic die a fiery death. After all, he found me, and I owed him a second chance. Hell, I wanted to give him a second chance. How could I refuse him when my body lit up like I had fireflies in my veins anytime I got within five feet of him or his silky voice?

He leaned forward and brushed my hair to the side. "The last time I looked at a calendar, a week consisted of seven days."

"Yeah. So?" I tensed my muscles to stave off the shiver that rolled through my body as his warm breath wafted over the microscopic hairs on my neck. It didn't work. Evidently, controlling involuntary body reactions was impossible.

"So, will you join me for lunch tomorrow?" he whispered.

With his lips a pesky inch from my ear, I nodded like a star struck groupie drinking in his mesmeric essence. Eyes wide. Mouth parted. Cheeks flushed. Pathetic.

"Good. So do you want to stay for another drink or go to dinner?" Archer asked. He propped his foot on the bottom rung of my barstool and the fabric of his pants brushed against my bare leg.

"Is something wrong with this place?" Winnie asked, smiling over the rim of her glass. I barely restrained the urge to roll my eyes. Here went her test.

His eyes darted toward Winnie. Then, he focused all his chocolaty, smoldering heat back on me. "It's not really my type of place, but if Langley wants to stay, I don't mind. Whatever Langley wants…" His voice trailed off, a suggestive smirk on his face. His lips were made for sweaty nights and sin.

"Thank God. Let's get out of this place." Winnie hopped out of her chair so fast, you'd think she'd won the lottery.

Archer chuckled. "Tell me how you really feel."

"Nine isn't our usual stomping ground," I said.

"I need to make reservations for dinner. Meet me outside in ten minutes." He handed me a fifty-dollar bill. "Will this cover it?"

I eyed the money. "You don't have to pay for our drinks."

Winnie snagged the money out of his hand. "If he's offering, who am I to reject his generosity?"

Archer's lips skimmed across my forehead. "See you in a couple minutes." I watched the back of his head. Even after he disappeared from my line of sight, I could pinpoint his location from the women's heads boomeranging in his direction.

"I'm taking off. You guys can go to dinner without me."

"What's wrong?" I asked, searching Winnie's eyes.

She smiled and leaned forward, so her mouth was inches from my ear. "I'm in the way. Archer likes you. I mean really likes you."

My heart tripped over itself. "How can you tell?"

"He ran all over town looking for you. He graciously agreed to hang out with you and your friend without complaint."

"I'm not sure. I thought Brandon liked me."

"No, Brandon liked the idea of you and what you could mean for his career."

"Maybe Archer feels the same way."

"Not even close. Have you seen the way he looks at you?" She fanned her face. "Within seconds of arriving, he had mentally undressed you at least twice.

I nearly choked on my drink. "Shut up."

"I'm jealous. It was like watching porn, but live."

"Did you really say that?"

"I did." She kissed me on the cheek as she squeezed my hand. "Have fun and fuck your stepdad."

I cringed. "Don't say that. I think my vodka just reversed course."

She rolled her eyes. "Not literally, but who cares what he thinks? He liked Brandon."

"So?"

"Brandon is like the head of the douche cavalry."

"The douche cavalry? Are you serious?"

She shrugged. "Hey, it sounded good in my head. Let's go find Archer and a taxi for me."

"Are you sure you don't want to come with us?" I leaned into her. "I don't mind. This was supposed to be a girls' night out."

She scrunched up her face. "Ah, yeah. I'm not lonely enough to spend a Friday night as the third wheel on your date with Mr. Dark, Sexy, and Filthy Rich."

CHAPTER TEN

Archer

"If you have a driver, why'd you take a taxi the night we met? Was it his night off or something?" Langley asked as she hopped into the backseat of the black town car. Her slim black skirt slid up her impressively toned legs.

I could've answered her question with a simple confirmation, or I could tell her the truth. I went with the truth. "I sent him home. I wanted to share a taxi with you."

Her eyes locked on mine, assessing, contemplating. I loosened my tie and pulled it over my head, dropping it on my briefcase. In the rush to find Langley, I hadn't bothered to stop home and change my clothes. When the silence lengthened, I braced for an inevitable sassy comment.

"I'm glad you did." She smiled. "So what do you have planned for dinner now that Winnie ditched us?"

I'd have to find a way to thank her friend

sometime in the future. I wasn't opposed to including Winnie in our dinner plans, but I preferred to be alone with Langley.

"Originally, I planned to take you to The Bar Café in Adams Morgan, but if you don't mind, I'd prefer to grab take-out and eat it at my place." Honestly, I should stick with the plan to meet her in public. I needed to push Senator Wharton, draw him out, and make him reckless. I couldn't do that by keeping my budding relationship with Langley secret, but I didn't want to be in public right now, and I had every reason to believe that Senator Wharton had someone trailing Langley anyway. Now that I thought about it, taking her to my house might be more effective than being photographed together.

"I'm not sure we're ready—"

I held up my hand, interrupting her train of thought the second her mind went *there*. Sure, if she wanted to go there, I was game, but I didn't want to risk having her crawling back into her shell and rejecting me entirely—not until I got what I wanted, what I needed. "I don't have an ulterior motive. It's been a long week, and, to be truthful, I'd rather spend time with you where we can relax." I ran my hand through my hair for the hundredth time since I walked out of my office in search of Langley. I'm pretty sure it had long since lost any style, and I resembled a mental patient more than number five on last year's D.C.'s most eligible bachelors list. Not that I cared, I hated that fucking title. I wished I'd gone with my initial gut instinct and refused to be part of the article. I didn't bust my ass to impress anyone else. I did it so I had the power to take down Senator Wharton when the time came.

"It was that bad, huh?"

"You can't imagine." I shook my head. "But let's not talk about work."

"Okay. Then, it's settled. We're eating take-out at your house."

"I'll make it up to you."

She shrugged. "Whatever. Spending time with you in private isn't a sacrifice."

A wholly unexpected sharp pain tugged at my chest. "Most women I've dated would disagree with you."

Her eyebrows lifted. "Then, you must have a habit of dating the wrong women."

"There might be more truth in that statement than I'd like to admit." I draped my arm over the back of the oyster-colored leather seat and pulled Langley closer to me. I didn't want to like her. It'd make everything I needed to do so much easier if I didn't like or respect her, but I didn't have a choice. Something about her called to me like no woman I'd ever met.

I should reevaluate and revise my plans. Wanting Langley like this was dangerous. She made me lose focus on the end goal. This entire week she had monopolized too many of my thoughts, and even after five days, my desire to call her, see her, and touch her hadn't faded.

"Hey," she said, rubbing her fingers between my eyebrows. She shifted closer so her leg pressed against mine from my hip to my knee. Her perfume invaded my senses, and her whisper-like touch lit up my nerve endings. "You're thinking too hard. Relax."

"Work stress," I murmured, distracted by the look on her face. Her eyes were soft. Her chin angled downward. Fuck, she looked like she cared...cared about me. I didn't remember the last time someone truly worried whether I was stressed, tired, or sad. Maybe mom had before she traveled so far down the road of self-pity she couldn't see anything but herself. Even before then, any respect and love she had for Knox and me came second to my mom's love of whiskey and amoral men. Except for Knox, the people in my life only valued what I could do for their career, their life, their bank account, or their social status.

Langley pulled her phone out of her purse. "Where do you live? I'll order us some food."

"There's a sushi restaurant in my building. It's convenient if you like sushi."

She twirled her phone in her grasp. "In your building? Where do you live? At a hotel?"

"Almost. The Residences at the Ritz-Carlton."

Her eyebrows scaled her forehead. "Why am I not surprised?"

"Hey." I squeezed her leg. "It's convenient. I split my time between New York and D.C. I don't the like maintenance that comes with owning a home, and the residences have a concierge, a maintenance service, and a valet."

"Well, aren't you special?" She scoffed, but her lips twitched with what I hoped was laughter and not disdain. "And I thought my two-bedroom townhome was impressive."

"I assure you, it was."

She elbowed the side of my ribcage. "You didn't see anything except the front door."

"And the kitchen," I reminded her. "But I wouldn't mind seeing a little more in the future." As I said the words, I realized the truth in that statement. I wanted to see more of Langley—her house, her friends, and everything that was important to her, which was dangerous. I needed to stop spinning fantasies about this woman, because the spark burning between us wouldn't mean anything when reality came knocking at our door, and it would happen sooner rather than later. Then, we'd be enemies for life. And being enemies with benefits wasn't a place I wanted to go with Langley, no matter the overwhelming attraction. After all, attraction faded and dulled with time no matter how hot it sizzled in the beginning. I hoped the shelf life on my fascination with Langley wasn't any different.

Simply put, I wanted to destroy the life she'd known for the last decade, dismantling it either brick by brick or with a bomb. It didn't matter to me as long as it ended with *his* complete disgrace and the loss of everything he held dear in his life. Langley wouldn't roll over and let me ruin her life and her family without a word. Our roles were scripted years ago, and nothing could alter it.

In spite of her gentle smiles, perfect curves, and toned to perfection legs, I had to keep everything in perspective. Ultimately, she was a spoiled rich girl with a famous actor, albeit deceased, for a dad, a social climbing bitch for a mother, and morally bankrupt stepdad. Her sweet demeanor and million dollar smile were a façade to get what she wanted.

To most women, I was nothing more than a healthy financial statement. Carefully crafted words wouldn't disguise the money signs twinkling in their jaded eyes. I couldn't let myself believe Langley was any different.

"I'd like that too," she said, leaning into me.

Off balance from my moody train of thought, it took me a moment to register her comment.

"Good." Forcing a smile on my face, I reached for the door handle when the car stopped next to the curb in front of the Ritz. "We're here."

CHAPTER ELEVEN

Langley

With the pricey address, I shouldn't have been surprised when I stepped into Archer's condo. The word condo didn't adequately describe the sleek elegance sprawling out in front of me. Muted whites, grays, silver, and accents of gold created a soothing palate. I expected dark, masculine colors that announced his bachelor status.

"This isn't what I expected." I dropped my purse on the glass table in the entry, complete with a white potted orchid.

"It's not?" he chuckled.

I rubbed my hands on the sides of my skirt as I absorbed every expertly coordinated detail. "No. It's beautiful, but it doesn't look lived in or personal."

"I know. I hired an interior designer friend, and I think she decorated as though she planned to move in someday. It's a little too feminine and sterile for my taste."

I sucked in a breath. His comment said more than I wanted to know about any of his previous entanglements. How pathetic. Jealousy slithered down my spine like the serpent tempting Eve with the forbidden fruit. I didn't have a right or reason to be jealous. We'd gone on a few dates that ended with a couple of kisses, hardly commitment material. My feelings weren't rational, but acknowledging that didn't make the unpleasant feeling in my gut any less real.

He tried to make eye contact. I avoided him as my gaze rolled over every item someone else had selected for him.

Golden starburst pillows.

A full-length walnut mirror propped against the entry wall.

The hammered silver coffee table cluster.

Meaningless leather bound books chosen for color not content.

"Maybe a little," I said breezily, trying to wash away any lingering uncomfortable feelings with my overly cheery tone. It didn't work.

Toying with the cuffs of his slightly wrinkled light-blue shirt, his dark eyes studied me. "I texted the concierge my normal order plus a couple things I thought you might like. He'll bring up our food in forty-five minutes or so, depending on how busy the restaurant is. Is that okay with you?"

"Sounds great," I said, my voice flat. I folded my arms across my chest and leaned against the waterfall stainless steel countertop on the kitchen island. When did I become so fragile that one little comment sent my confidence into a downward spiral?

I turned away as he sauntered toward me. A medley of aqua glass and stainless tiles ran the length of the backsplash. The glare of the incandescent lighting reflected from the shiny materials, creating little starbursts of light on the medium-brown horizontal grained cabinets.

"Did the comment about the interior designer upset you?"

My cheeks heated. "Not really. I have thick skin. Don't worry about me." It was the truth. Living with my mom forced me to grow a tortoise-like shell around my heart. I hated that he pierced it so easily. "Besides, it isn't my business. We hardly know each other."

"That's not what I asked."

I ran my finger over the smooth countertop, still not meeting his heavy gaze. "It's not important."

His hands looped around my waist, and he pulled my back against his chest. His spicy scent infiltrated the air around me, ensuring I couldn't ignore him even if his touch didn't do the trick.

"Truly, she was only a friend. I suspected she wanted more, and that's why she's not part of my life anymore. If it annoys you, I'll change some of the stuff in here, make it more mine."

I spun within the confines of his arms. "That's silly. You don't have to do that for a woman you just met. They're just things, and if you don't think they mean anything, I believe you."

He cradled my face with his long-fingered hands like I was precious cargo, and even if his eyes weren't smoldering with desire, I would've been a goner. When was the last time someone looked at me like that? Like they wanted me. Like I was special. Like I was worth the trouble. Maybe never, or maybe it had been so long that it seemed like never.

"It's not a big deal. I don't love everything anyway, and I want you to be comfortable at my place, not turning every corner imagining another woman's dreams in everything you see."

His lashes lowered, and all of his concentration focused on me with swoon-worthy attention to detail, thawing me from the inside out. At that instant, I realized I was in trouble—in trouble of really falling for Archer. My heart raced and my hands trembled as I circled my arms around his waist, beneath his suit jacket but over his shirt.

One hand still cupped my face as he tangled the other one into my hair. We stood frozen in painful anticipation, his mouth hovering inches from mine, and then he kissed me gently, lovingly even, one beautiful brush of his lips at a time. His lips were warm, and his breath smelled minty. I wanted to taste more of him…all of him.

My tongue darted out of my mouth, licking the seam of his lips. Then, without a second to process the consequence of my actions, the kiss tumbled into a frantic tug of war that successfully wiped my mind of any kiss I had shared with any other man before Archer. Stroke by stroke, we consumed each other.

Nothing compared.

Nothing came close.

Our tongues danced in perfect synchronicity as

though we were created for each other. We couldn't get deep enough. We couldn't get close enough, but it didn't stop me from trying to feed the lust burning inside of me like I stood on the threshold of the second circle of hell.

We pushed and pulled at each other, desperate to purge even one centimeter of distance between our bodies. I tugged at the hem of his shirt and ripped it from the waistband of his pants, burrowing my hands underneath the material. My blunt cut nails scored the rope-like muscles along his spine. My innate internal defenses hadn't merely lowered; they had plummeted shamelessly and uncontrollably like a meteor caught in the earth's gravitational field.

Archer's hand traced the side of my face, my neck, my collarbone, only stopping his exploratory descent when he reached the side of my breast. His lips coasted to my neck, nibbling, tasting, and licking. Like a well-orchestrated magic trick, my body responded to his non-verbal commands. Goosebumps showered my arms. My nipples tightened, and my breath stuck in my throat before whooshing out in one giant leap that suspiciously resembled a moan.

Ding.

The noise hardly penetrated my Archer-induced fog of lust. My hands fumbled with the top button of his shirt as my eyes locked on his face, savoring every angle of his savagely beautiful face, taut with desire. I wanted, needed, and craved every part of him, and I was long past caring about the repercussions. One button, two buttons, and then three, and my eyes raked over the sinful expanse of his chest exposed for my viewing pleasure.

Ding.

Then, it was his turn. He slid my shirt up, but didn't limit himself to looking. His lips sealed over my lace-covered nipple. My eyes fluttered closed, and I arched my back, drowning in the all-consuming burst of pleasure. My world narrowed on him, on us, and each and every stroke and suck of his too skilled mouth. Wobbly, lightheaded, I clung to him, basking in the sensations he lured so effortlessly from my all too willing body.

Ding.

"Shit," Archer said, stepping away from me, rubbing his hands along the sides of his thighs.

"What?" I said, my body sagging. Without the countertop behind me for support, I would've tumbled to the floor. My breath exited my lungs in jagged, uneven pants.

"The food."

Dizzy and out of focus, my mind spun, unraveling his words as though he had spoken Sanskrit instead two simple English words.

Food?

What food?

Crap, the sushi Archer ordered.

No, no, no. I had never hated sushi as much as I did at that moment. I didn't want anything to interrupt where we were headed. I wanted to continue the plunge into the world where only Archer and I existed. My fingers dove into my hair, raking the tangled strands away from my face. "Right. Sushi."

He closed the distance between us again and

stroked the skin of my lower lip, the brief touch almost unbearable when he had no intention of continuing his attentions.

"Don't look so disappointed, Langley." His hand dropped and he walked backward toward the front door. "The night isn't over yet."

His promise was a double-edged sword. I wanted more of what Archer offered, but part of me wanted to hold Archer at bay a little longer, testing the waters before I dove in with reckless abandon. He'd steal my heart without trying, and I didn't know if he'd offer his in return.

Since my dad died, love seemed like a commodity in short supply. My mom cared. Maybe my stepdad did too, but I could never quite convince myself that either of them loved me in the same unconditional all-encompassing way my dad did. More often than not, I felt like a prop in their Norman Rockwell audition on the never-ending campaign trail rather than a treasured member of the Wharton family.

If I gave into Archer and our relationship soured, he'd break what little spirit I had left after that Brandon debacle.

CHAPTER TWELVE

Archer

After we ate dinner, Langley fell asleep on my couch halfway through some chick flick she forced me to watch. The best and safest option would involve waking her up and arranging my car service to shuttle her back to her house, but I had no intention of doing that. I wasn't ready to let her go.

Curled into a ball with her arms cradling a pillow, her long golden hair framed her face with soft waves. She looked almost angelic. She was the perfect combination of her dad's famous golden coloring and her mom's petite, delicate features.

I pulled the gray throw blanket over her legs and retreated to my study to touch base with Knox. At my desk, I popped open the bottle of Ibuprofen stashed in the middle drawer and washed three pills down with the last sip of my wine.

I rubbed the back of my neck and then called Knox. It was well past midnight, but Knox would answer my call. He always did.

"Knox, it's Archer."

"I know who it is. I have caller ID on my cell phone like the rest of the world. Besides, you're the only person who wouldn't think twice about calling me this late."

"I think I'm the only person who calls you." I leaned back in my chair. Knox had tons of acquaintances, but not many friends. The women he dated rarely made it beyond date three. Knox joked that after three dates they expected things like a relationship and gifts. He didn't want anything permanent, so he cut them loose before the demands started accumulating.

"True. So how'd the date go?" Knox asked, his voice sounding more awake than ten seconds earlier.

"Technically, it's still going," I replied dryly.

Knox chuckled. "I'm impressed. I guess that part of your plan is progressing smoothly. You're lucky she isn't hard on the eyes, otherwise you would've had to lower your standards."

"It's not what you're thinking. She fell asleep. I don't want to wake her." Truthfully, if she hadn't fallen asleep, I had every intention of continuing where we left off before the food delivery interrupted us.

"Since when are you chivalrous?" he said sarcastically.

"Are you finished, or you still trying to make a point?"

"As a matter of fact, I do have a point to make."

"And what's that?" I responded, pinching the bridge of my nose.

"I think you should focus on Senator Wharton and leave Langley out of your plans."

"Did you have a sudden attack of conscience? Why the hell would I do that?"

"Because you like her," he said belatedly, his voice tentative.

An image of Langley swam before my over-tired eyes. "You're wrong," I snapped, even though both of us knew it was a blatant lie. I more than liked Langley, which explained why I'd spent the better part of the week avoiding her and two hours tracking her down tonight when it looked like she wanted to end things.

Every time Knox asked about Langley this week, I nearly ripped his head off. I didn't want to talk about her. My feelings were messy and complicated. I needed her to get to Senator Wharton, but I also wanted her for reasons wholly unrelated to him.

To make matters worse, after meeting her last weekend, I felt ridiculously possessive and protective of her, which wasn't a good sign, because destroying Senator Wharton would mean ripping her life apart. I wish things were different, that Senator Wharton wasn't part of either of our lives, but no amount of wishing would alter reality.

She wouldn't want anything to do with me when I exposed Senator Wharton and destroyed his political career, and the idea of Langley hating me left a sour taste in my mouth. Even though I knew it was for the best, my gut hollowed at the loss of something I could never have. If I were smart, I wouldn't touch her or make love to her—something

I wanted more with each passing second I spent with her.

"Am I?"

"Absolutely. She's attractive. She's an above average conversationalist, but she's related to *him*." And that was exactly why I needed to kill any emotional investment I had in Langley before it got out of hand.

"Fine."

Grateful he didn't press the issue, my shoulders relaxed. "Tell me about the surveillance."

"Senator Wharton has someone keeping loose tabs on Langley, but he's not actively watching you. In fact, you don't even register on his radar."

"What do you mean by loose?"

"Nothing intrusive. A car follows her to and from work. Tonight, the car followed her to the bar and then to the front of your building." Knox's experience and connections from his time in Naval Intelligence were invaluable.

I twirled the stem of my empty wine glass. "Is the car still outside my place right now?"

"I don't know. I went to bed an hour ago. I can reach out to our surveillance team now, or I can wait to review the emailed report in the morning. Which would you prefer?"

"Tomorrow will work. Nothing's going to happen tonight anyway."

"Nope." The silence echoed through the phone. "Which makes me wonder the real reason you woke me up in the middle of the night."

"I know where you're going with this, and I've had enough."

"Where am I going?"

"You're circling the conversation back to Langley," I retorted.

"I think we should focus on Senator Wharton. We don't need Langley. He has plenty of career-ending skeletons hidden in his closet. We'll be able to uncover a big one in no time. I've been investigating his connections to the financier the FBI arrested last month. I think there's something there."

"I know there's something there, but I don't want Senator Wharton to be the next President of the United States by the time the pieces come together. If we can't stop his election, every piece of evidence we uncover will be buried under miles of administrative tape, and he'll have every governmental agency under the sun climbing up my ass the minute he's sworn into office. The SEC, IRS, DEA, FBI—you name it. They'll all be clamoring for a piece of Black Investments and me. It'd be a fucking mess." I rubbed my temples as I contemplated the nightmarish implications of a Wharton presidency.

"So what do you want to do?"

"I want to explore every angle and I'll make a final decision later. In the meantime, put a tail on Langley too. Maybe we're missing something." Indecision normally wasn't a problem for me. When I started this whole thing, I wanted to ruin Senator Wharton and everyone in his life, which naturally included Langley. But that was before I met her, tasted her, caressed her golden skin, and craved her more than my next breath. Before I'd seen the mixed reaction, both sadness and hate, swirl in her emerald eyes at the mention of Senator Wharton's name.

To make matters more complicated, she was sweet, nice even. Way too fucking good for me. Instead of spending the last four years living off her stepdad, waist-deep in the life of a socialite, she put her degree and training to work. She accepted an entry-level physical therapist position. Most people with millions of dollars banked in a trust fund wouldn't live off a low-paying job when thirty years old was right around the corner.

She didn't deserve my hatred, and she certainly didn't deserve to be used. But was I actually using her? It sure as hell didn't feel that way. If my inability to stop thinking about her was any indication, I wasn't. I groaned inwardly. I needed to focus on the end goal, not my need for Langley.

"Got it," Knox finally replied. "Call me tomorrow."

CHAPTER THIRTEEN

Langley

Nothing looked familiar. My eyes traveled around the room, trying to pinpoint my location. Dimmed sconces lit the linear angles of a white marble fireplace. A gray chenille blanket covered my legs. Shit. I must have fallen asleep at Archer's house, and he was nowhere to be found. I guess he went to bed.

I lifted my phone off the metal coffee table. It was a little after one in the morning. I didn't know if I should look for him, or leave and shoot him a text when I got home. Neither option appealed to me. Why the hell did I fall asleep?

I had folded the blanket, draped it over the arm of the sofa, and rearranged the pillows when I noticed a sliver of yellow light squeezing under the door on the far side of the room. Without over thinking my actions, I crossed the room and knocked on the closed door.

"You can come in," Archer said.

I cracked the door and peeked inside. Archer sat in a gray leather chair behind a sable-stained desk. A gray and white Moroccan-inspired rug covered the hardwood floors.

"I'm sorry I fell asleep," I said, taking a few hesitant steps into the room.

He leaned back in his chair. "No problem. I had some work to finish up."

My gaze drifted to the white floor-to-ceiling bookshelves behind his oversized desk. "I'm just…" I caught my lips with my teeth, and then swallowed hard. What the hell was I doing? Since when did a man turn me into a tongue-tied fool? "I'm just gonna go."

"Come here," he said, beaconing me with a simple wave of his hand.

When I reached the corner of his desk, I balanced my hip against the sharp edge. "Yes?"

"Were you planning to leave without bothering to give me a goodnight kiss?"

"I didn't think about it," I murmured.

Less than a fragment of a second later, his hands circled my hips, and he tugged me into his lap. My face mere inches from his, I smelled his intoxicating spicy-citrus scent, and I saw the desire swirling in his dilated pupils. I wanted to kiss him. No, I wanted more than a kiss this time.

Clutching the top of his shoulders, I pressed my lips against his, taking what I wanted for once in my life without weighing all the implications of my actions. I'd spent the first twenty-four years of my life making decisions based on how they affected my family, but that hadn't gotten me anything except a string of boyfriends, each one shittier than the previous one. This reckless and impulsive moment was about me, and I wanted Archer. My stepdad and his fucking campaign be damned.

His hands ran up and down my back, slowly shifting me closer and closer to him until we were chest-to-chest, pelvis-to-pelvis, and our lips met, melding us together like two pieces of a puzzle. Our tongues tangled and curled around each other in a kiss that was more hello than goodbye.

Within seconds, my body was on fire, aching to take the next step. My skin stretched tight, anticipating his next move, and I didn't have to wait long.

In one swoop, he stood up, wrapping my legs around his waist, and carried me down the hall. With every step, I kissed his throat, his cheek, his ear…anything within striking range of my Archer-starved lips.

"Will you stay?" he asked, sliding my body down the length of his until my bare feet touched the thick weave of the carpet.

"I want to stay, but I'm nervous," I admitted. The reality of being with him, sleeping in his bed, and waking up next to him rushed through me. It would make our relationship real in the way a few kisses and dates never could.

He cocked his head to the side and traced the lines of my face. "Don't be. I want you to stay, and I think you want to stay. We're not doing anything wrong."

I blew out a puff of air. "You're right." Standing on the tips of my toes, I kissed the side of his throat as my hands worked the buttons of his shirt.

"You first," he mumbled, pushing my hands away. He tugged my shirt over my head and unhooked the back of my bra. With a feather-soft swipe of his fingers, he slid one strap down my arm, then the other, and my bra tumbled to the floor. His hands cupped my bare breasts and a simultaneous shiver and jolt of fire shot through my body.

I closed my eyes as my nipples pebbled under his caresses. Around and around, his fingers explored the contours of my breasts, plucking and rolling them between his finger and thumb until my breath came in short pants and my heart winged against my ribcage.

When his mouth closed over one nipple, my knees buckled and my nipples throbbed in time with my heartbeat. "Oh my God," I whispered. "This is so unfair."

Chuckling, he eased me onto the top of his bed. "How so?" He unzipped my skirt and slid it down my legs, the tips of his fingers igniting mini-shocks with every graze along my over-sensitized flesh.

My eyes popped open. "For starters, you could take off your shirt so I don't feel so naked."

"Soon," he said. He dropped to his knees between my already parted legs and glanced up at me from under the thick fall of his dark forelock.

His hands stroked the inside of my thighs and then his mouth followed at a torturous pace. I fisted the duvet as his lips and fingers ambled higher and higher. By the time he reached the silken edge of my panties, I'd thought I might explode with one simple wisp of his warm breath.

And then he kissed me through my panties. I moaned, or maybe I screamed. I arched my hips against him. He ripped my panties down my legs, and within seconds he was licking and sucking me with expert precision. I was drunk on pleasure...drunk on him. I rocked my hips against him, selfishly seeking the release burning just out of my reach.

He slid two fingers inside of me, and it was too good, too perfect, too everything. Time crawled, almost freeze-framing, as every nerve-ending aligned and every muscle flexed. Then, I shattered, bowing my hips, pressing against him, channeling my pleasure into his mouth with every tantalizing vibration.

Archer pulled his shirt over his head and shoved his pants and boxer briefs down his legs. A beautifully naked body stood over me, and I wondered how many other women have been lucky enough to see him like this. A flat toned stomach, defined legs and arms, and a small trail of dark hair stretching from his navel to his impressive erection.

Oh my God, I inspected him as though I'd never seen a naked man before, which in some respects was true. I had never been intimate with a man who compared to him. Brandon ran almost daily, but his body was wiry, and not in the same league as Archer's. An image of me snapping a picture of him like this so I could study every detail in the privacy of my home flickered through my mind. I bit my lip to stifle my laughter. What a silly thought.

"Like what you see?" he smiled, flashing a small dimple in his right cheek. I'd never noticed it before.

Spellbound, I nodded.

He opened the bedside table and pulled out a condom. Within seconds, he rolled it over his length and braced his body over mine. He rubbed his erection along my sex, and I went from satisfied to desperate in ten seconds flat.

"Please," I muttered more to myself than him, but he complied. He pushed inside of me one taunting inch, but he held back. How could he be so disciplined when my control was within a hairsbreadth of snapping? I was the one who had an orgasm not less than five minutes ago, not him. I'd impale myself on him if he'd let me, but the look in his eyes told me he was the director of this journey, and I was only along for the ride.

"Not enough," I moaned.

"Trust me. I'm just getting started."

Then, he slammed all the way inside of me, hard, deep, and absolutely moan-worthy. His hands circled my hips, and he angled my hips, somehow managing to plant his cock even deeper than two seconds earlier. I hooked my legs around his waist, using my ankles to force him to move...and move he did.

I didn't even have time to revel in the new angle before he started pumping in and out of me with wicked accuracy. His hands roamed freely, not leaving any part of my body untouched or neglected. Moonlight lit the sharp-angled planes of his face.

When his fingers teased my clit, I should've been embarrassed that I was ready to orgasm again, but my pleasure-filled synapses were firing too fast for the thought to take root. My hips moved restlessly against his, up, down, and circling without any finesse. My entire body throbbed in rhythm with my rapid-fire heartbeat.

Desperate sounds escaped my parted lips as sensations in my core built and built to tidal wave proportions. Then, his mouth crashed against mine, kissing me. Sinfully. Frantically. With absolute domination. All tongue and teeth, connecting us in every way possible until we were one body moving together. I couldn't touch him enough. The hunger was too overwhelming.

Like a lightning bolt straight to my heart, ecstasy flooded my body surpassing anything I'd ever experienced. Then, a split second later he hit a place I never realized existed, and I exploded. Not even missing a beat, Archer swallowed my cries of bliss and continued to thrust inside of me, any ounce of restraint long since gone.

With the aftershocks of my climax still tingling in the tips of my fingers and my toes, he came with one hard thrust and a harsh groan. When I finally opened my eyes, Archer was still buried inside of me with his forehead resting against mine.

"I liked that version of a goodnight kiss. We'll have to do that more often," I said, my voice a delicate whisper.

He kissed me on the lips before rolling off of me. "I concur."

My eyes already heavy with sleep, I turned my head to face his. "Do you still want me to stay?"

"I do." His mouth curved in amusement as he

gathered me into his arms, and there was that familiar dimple again.

Lazily, I traced his dimple. "My stepdad has one exactly like this," I said more to myself than him. "Isn't that strange?"

He flinched, and his hand curled into a ball against my back.

"Sorry." I searched his dark, almost predatory eyes for a strained moment. "Poor choice of conversation," I finally said.

"Not the best." He blew out a breath and kissed my lips tenderly. "Let's go to sleep."

CHAPTER FOURTEEN

Langley

Golden hued, mid-morning sun snuck through the cracks of the blinds when I opened my eyes. Not ready to face the day, I rolled to my side and wrapped the pinstriped pillow over my head. I needed to get up, but exhaustion from a long night in Archer's arms made me too lazy to behave responsibly.

"Finally," Archer said, the bed dipping next to my hip. "I didn't peg you for a late sleeper."

I groaned, not bothering to remove the pillow from my face. "Why are you awake?"

"It's eleven thirty. I haven't slept past eight thirty since I turned twenty-one."

I popped up in the bed. Thank God I texted my mom yesterday to cancel our weekly tennis match. "Eleven thirty? What the hell? Why did you let me sleep for so long?"

"You looked comfortable, and I had to work."

"Ugh." I rubbed my eyes with my palms and

then dropped my hands into my lap. Black streaks of mascara colored my skin. "I need a shower. I'm a mess."

He kissed my forehead. "Not even close."

"No need to lie. I'll just wash my face and then I'll be out of your way."

"Shower here. I made a late breakfast."

"You mean lunch?" I said, pointing at the alarm clock.

"Exactly. I owe you lunch, but I can't go out because something came up."

"Work stuff?" I stretched my arms over my head.

He looked over his shoulder. "A meeting."

"Okay. I'll clean up, and we can eat in about thirty minutes. Will that work?"

"Perfect. I hope you like waffles."

"I love waffles."

I watched him leave the room. Then, I scooped up my clothes and purse from the ivory leather chair in the corner and carried them into the bathroom. The bathroom was decorated in the same white and gray theme as the rest of the house. Carrara marble in several sizes covered the floors and walls of the bathroom. Three walls of glass enclosed a shower that could fit at least five people comfortably.

The minute I turned on the shower, my phone rang. *Shit*. I never called Winnie after we left the bar. She was probably going crazy with a combination of curiosity and worry.

"Hi," I said without looking at the screen.

"Langley, it's Brandon."

My heart squeezed and I nearly dropped the phone. He was the last person I wanted to talk to right now, or ever for that matter. "Why the hell are you calling me?"

"I'm sorry about last week…at the bar. The way I acted wasn't acceptable. You didn't deserve that."

"You're right. And that's exactly why I'm hanging up the phone. Don't call me back. Ever."

"Wait," Brandon said, as I pulled the phone away from my ear. "Don't hang up."

"We don't have anything to talk about," I yelled, not even bothering to press the phone against my ear.

"*He* knows."

"Excuse me?" My hands shook like I desperately needed coffee. I couldn't catch my breath. My stomach dropped to the floor. My blood roared in my ears. My vision swam. I was going to have a panic attack in the middle of Archer's bathroom.

"Langley, he knows," he repeated, his voice dropping to a raspy whisper.

"I don't get it. How?" I bent over the countertop, staring at my crazed reflection in the mirror. My skin looked pasty. My eyes blinked wildly. My hair resembled a beehive.

"At first, I thought you told him—"

"I didn't," I interrupted. If I had my choice, I'd never confront my stepdad about the information in that email. In fact, if I could pay someone to scrub my mind of the event, I would seriously consider it. Reading those two paragraphs was toxic to my health. When I scanned the first sentence, I knew I should've stopped reading, but I didn't listen to my gut. By the time I realized the depth of my stupidity, Brandon stood over my shoulder.

"I know."

"Then how?"

"We can't talk about this over the phone."

"Do you want to come to my house later?"

"God no. Your house could be bugged."

My lungs constricted momentarily. Then, my heart accelerated as though someone injected me with adrenaline. "You're crazy," I said, accompanied by a half-laugh that resembled a cough. Over the last ten years, my stepdad had done a lot of not so great stuff, but I wanted to believe I was immune from his scorch the earth philosophy.

"Meet me in front of the Lincoln Memorial in two hours. We'll take a stroll and then part ways."

I hesitated. I didn't like the idea of being alone with Brandon, particularly after our last encounter. I couldn't drag Winnie into this mess, and as much as I liked Archer, I wasn't 100 percent certain I could trust him. Not because he was untrustworthy or bad, but because the information was too sensitive. Too explosive.

"Fine. I'll meet you, but I can't make it there until three."

"Why?"

"I'm busy, and my life isn't your business anymore."

"You need to be careful who you trust."

I raked my hands through my hair, tugging on the ends. "I know that. I'm not dumb. I may not live and breathe politics like you, but I have learned a thing or two over the last decade."

"I'm just trying to protect you," he answered, sounding relieved. He cleared his throat. "And I

111

don't trust that guy from the bar."

"Archer?" I sat down on the rectangular, slotted teak bench outside the shower.

There was an awkward pause on the phone. "Yes, him."

"You don't know him," I said absently, my imagination running wild with the implications of my stepfather knowing I read that email.

"I don't, but something about him is familiar, and not in a good way."

"Because he attended the fundraiser that night."

"Maybe," he answered, but he didn't sound convinced. Either way, I couldn't think about that right now. I had bigger things to worry about.

"I'll see you at three." I hung up the phone before he could say anything else to ruin the day that held so much promise less than twenty minutes ago.

Archer knocked on the door, and I nearly jumped out of my skin. "Langley?"

The door handle rattled. Thank God I had locked the door. I couldn't face him now.

"Yes."

"The food is ready. Are you almost done?"

"Give me fifteen more minutes," I answered, slipping my phone back into my purse and pressing the heel of my hand against the door. Thick white steam from the shower filled the bathroom, and I could no longer see my reflection in the mirror.

"Are you okay?" He shifted against the door.

"I'm fine." Did my voice sound normal? I couldn't be sure. Brandon warned me not to trust Archer, but I knew better than to trust anything

Brandon said. Like everyone in Washington, Brandon had a self-serving agenda, but what about Archer? Did he have an ulterior motive? I didn't know. I was falling for him, but I refused to allow my emotions to cloud my judgment. There was too much at stake.

CHAPTER FIFTEEN

Archer

"She's hiding something," I said the minute Knox sat down at the table. He had texted me this morning asking to meet me for coffee. After having a small taste of Langley, I had preferred to spend the day with her, making the most of every minute we had together, but Knox wouldn't relent.

"Who?" Knox dropped a folder on the white round table.

"Langley. Who else?"

Knox raised one eyebrow and folded his arms across the planes of his checked shirt. "You're hiding something too. It only seems appropriate. Don't you think?"

"Sure." I took a drawn out sip of my lukewarm coffee. "It's certainly ironic, or something like that, but I need her to trust me if this is going to work. I need information." Clearly, she was accustomed to handling her problems on her own, but I wanted her to feel comfortable confiding in me, and not just because I needed information.

"Trust takes time. You don't trust her. Why should she trust you?" he said smoothly.

"Can you stifle your compulsion to be rational and listen to me?"

"When you grow up with a politician as skilled at masking his true intentions as Senator Wharton, a lot more than money and nepotism rub off on you."

"She's planning to meet Brandon today," I confessed, and it felt like a confession because I almost didn't want to share this information with Knox. I couldn't stand the thought of her being complicit in or tainted by Senator Wharton's mountain of lies. I shouldn't care. The obstacles to us having a real relationship were varied and numerous on both of our sides. She just didn't know any of that yet, but she would soon enough. Too bad my body didn't give a fuck about any of that the second I came within a hundred feet of her.

After she fell asleep last night, I stared at the ceiling, searching for a loophole in the predetermined end of our relationship. I needed her in my life long enough to eliminate the clawing need to touch her and kiss her. Hours later, I still didn't have a satisfactory solution.

"How do you know?"

I leaned back in my chair. "I overheard the end of their phone conversation this morning."

"Where?"

"I'm not sure, but she's meeting him at three."

Knox's fingers glided along the screen of his phone. "I've got someone on it."

I tapped my fingers on the top of the worn wood

table.

"Could you hear anything else she said?" Knox asked.

"Not a lot. She was in the bathroom with the shower running."

Knox rubbed his jaw. "Do you think she's still involved with him?"

"No," I answered automatically, even as anger and suspicion churned in my gut. Maybe she and Brandon were working together. When Brandon confronted her at the bar that night, both their comments were cryptic and vague, but anyone with ears could tell something wasn't right. My desire for her had obliterated my common sense. "Dammit. I don't know."

"Well, I guess all we can do is wait and see how this unfolds, unless..." His voice trailed off.

"Unless what?"

"Unless you want to forget this whole thing and bury the past once and for all."

I stood up and smiled grimly. "I wish it were that simple, but I can't do it. He ruined my life and our mom's life."

Knox shook his head. "He didn't ruin your life. Your childhood, yes, but not your life. And mom...she made bad decisions before and after she met him. He contributed to her downfall, but she had a hand in it too. A big hand."

He was right. We both knew it, but she had never admitted it. She blamed everyone but herself for her problems. Self-reflection wasn't her thing. "Do you think he had anything to do with her death?" It wasn't the first time the thought crossed my mind, but I'd never given voice to my suspicion before. My gut had guided me through plenty of ugly moments. Whether it was abuse by another one of my mom's drunken boyfriends or making the right investment, I relied on my intuition to point me in the right direction. From the day I learned she killed herself, I had a hard time believing the facts presented by the police.

He shifted in his seat. "The police ruled her death a suicide," he said, but I heard a note of disbelief in his voice.

My mind reeled as I gazed out the window of the coffee shop. The sidewalk was thick with people. A couple of children darted ahead of their mom, laughing. A man gestured wildly while he yelled into his phone.

"I don't believe it. I never have," I said after a moment. "She finally started putting her life together, and she wasn't drinking anymore. She found a job. It doesn't make sense that she'd do all that work just to put a bullet in her brain two months later."

He twisted his coffee cup on the table. "No, it doesn't, but I haven't found any clear and convincing evidence to the contrary." His voice was measured, calm even.

My stomach lurched into my throat, choking me. "But you suspect something, don't you?"

"Yes," he said.

Knox was a natural strategist with a criminal attorney's affinity for investigation. Since we were kids, he loved dismantling lies and half-truths— sometimes with investigative work, sometimes with

Machiavellian planning—which explained his first career as an intelligence officer in the navy. To this day, he hadn't changed. If evidence existed suggesting foul play in our mother's death, he'd find it.

"And you still think we should stop digging into Senator Wharton's life?"

Knox stood up and braced his hands on the table. "It'd be the safest thing to do, but neither of us ever take the easy way out."

I smiled. "So why start now?"

"My sentiments exactly. I'll have our team look through Langley's home while she's out with Brandon."

"Make sure they put everything back in order. I don't want her to suspect anything." I rubbed the back of my neck. "And make sure Senator Wharton's team doesn't catch them in the act."

Knox smirked. "It shouldn't be a problem. This isn't my first rodeo."

"I know."

He glanced at his watch as though he had somewhere to go, and he probably did. He worked for Black Investments in security, but I didn't have any illusions that it was his only gig. I didn't ask him for particulars anymore. Based on his tight-lipped responses, I assumed he still did contract work for the government in an unofficial capacity, but he never shared the details, probably because he couldn't.

"I have another meeting. If it works for you, I'll touch base tonight with more information."

"Of course."

CHAPTER SIXTEEN

Langley

Wind whipped hair around my face as I crossed Lincoln Memorial Circle and approached the steps in front of the monument. Wrapped in a long, black overcoat, Brandon stood on one of the steps in front of me. He lifted a hand in acknowledgment and jogged down the stairs to meet me.

"Let's circle the reflection pool." He pressed his hand into my back, guiding me back across Lincoln Memorial.

"Fine." I quickened my pace, and his hand slipped from my back. "Tell me what's going on," I said, cutting to the point of our meeting. I didn't want to spend any more time than necessary in his company.

"Last week I was going through some files."

"Yeah?" I stuffed my hands into the pockets of my cream jacket.

Brandon glanced over his shoulder. "Wait. Before we discuss this, I need to look at your phone."

I stopped walking. "No."

"Just let me see it. I think Senator Wharton is monitoring your calls."

I slid the phone out of my pocket and scanned the front and back. "Looks fine to me."

Brandon snatched it out of my hand. "Does the battery drain quickly?"

"Lately, yes, but I'm due for an upgrade."

He removed the gray hard-shelled cover from my phone and dismantled the battery. "The battery is hot to the touch."

"So what?" I said, holding out my hand.

"So, he has someone monitoring your phone. Mine too." He dropped the pieces of my phone into my open hand. "Keep the battery out of it until you can buy a new phone. Change your number too."

"Why?"

"You'll be harder to track."

"I can't keep my phone number secret from my family." I put my hands on my hips. "Tell me what the fuck is going on."

Brandon threaded his fingers through his blond hair. "Remember how Senator Wharton asked me to research those ten women?"

I tipped my head toward the sky, letting the late afternoon sunshine wash over my face. "I remember."

He nodded. "As you gathered from that email, Senator Wharton had an intimate relationship with every one of them at some point in the last thirty years."

"Right. You said as much six months ago," I

snapped. "He wanted you to convince them to sign a nondisclosure agreement in exchange for money as a preventative measure before he announced his plan to run for president."

He rubbed his hands together in front of his chest. "Only seven of the ten signed the agreement."

"Obviously he did something to convince the remaining three to be quiet. He plans to announce his candidacy next week. He wouldn't do that if there were any loose ends."

"The three holdouts are dead."

A shiver ran down my spine. "Did they die recently?"

"All of them died within a week of their refusal to sign the agreement."

My stomach flipped. "Surely, it's a coincidence," I said, but knee-jerk emotion rather than logic caused me to utter those words.

Brandon shrugged. "All three deaths were ruled suicides if that makes you feel any better."

I nodded absently, staring at trees as the wind rattled their bare branches. They seemed more sinister than a minute earlier. "It wouldn't make sense to kill those women. Lots of politicians have affairs. It's not as big of a deal as it was ten or fifteen years ago. He wasn't married during all of them either."

Brandon kicked a pebble off the sidewalk into the reflection pool. "You're right, but the circumstances of Senator Wharton's affairs are slightly different."

"How so?"

"All of his affairs occurred when the women

were under the age of eighteen. They were highly paid escorts."

"What?" I whispered, the word ringing unnaturally in my ears. "I don't understand."

"Gerald Whittaker. Does the name sound familiar?"

"Yes. He's the self-made billionaire the FBI arrested last month, but I haven't followed the story closely. I don't know any details."

"Nobody does. Well, not yet anyway, but maybe never if Senator Wharton gets his way." Brandon shoved his hands into the pockets of his overcoat.

"What am I missing?"

"Gerald has been so successful because he does favors for important people."

"What kind of favors?"

"He provides things they can't seek out themselves."

"Like?"

Brandon glanced over his shoulder. "Investigators claim Gerald trafficked and traded sexual favors from several bought-and-paid-for underage females, some of them as young as twelve, and loaned them out to his friends and corrupt politicians."

My eyebrows knitted together. "What does he get out of it?"

"Power. The ability to extract favors from these people at a later date in the form of votes, favorable land deals, and other things."

My mouth dropped open. Could people really be so stupid? They had to realize they stepped into a trap. "Like blackmail?"

Brandon rubbed his hands over his face. "Exactly like that."

I couldn't say anything. My lips froze even as my mind whirled with the implications of Brandon's disclosure.

Six months ago, I thought Brandon and my stepdad wanted to cover his extramarital affairs both during his current marriage and with his first wife. I ended our relationship because Brandon was complicit in harboring lies that kept my mom in the dark and effectively chained her to my stepdad.

I couldn't fathom how he sat at the dinner table with us every Sunday and chatted with my mom while maintaining a straight face. Maybe my mom wouldn't end her marriage. After all, she craved the power too, but at least she had the ability to make an intelligent choice.

I rubbed my temples. "And Gerald Whittaker apparently had something to do with the ten women connected to Senator Wharton?"

Brandon rocked back on his heels. "From what I've gathered, he introduced Senator Wharton to all of those women. From murmurings on the Hill, Whittaker kept evidence of the encounters as insurance. Pictures. Videos. The FBI uncovered some evidence from his computer, but the case is moving slowly. Probably because the evidence will rock more than one politician's career."

"What does this have to do with me?"

"Senator Wharton and many other people are anxious for this information to disappear, and you have information you shouldn't."

"Until this moment, I didn't know much. I saw a

list of women's names, most of which I don't remember. I didn't even finish reading the email. Thomas wanted them to sign something agreeing to keep their relationships secret." I shrugged. "Big deal." I didn't add that I printed a copy of the email and hid it in my coat pocket before I left. I couldn't explain why I did it. I haven't looked at it since that day, except to hide it in a box in my closet, but for some reason I thought I might need it in the future. Evidently, I made the right decision.

"They don't know that. If I hadn't ripped the iPad out of your hand, you would know more." He grabbed my upper arms and lowered his voice. "I discovered a listening device in my home a couple weeks after we broke up. I assume it's been there for a long time. Plus, I've heard things I wasn't meant to hear."

"Like what?"

"That's all I can tell you, but don't fool yourself. They are watching you. Everything you say and everywhere you go is reported to Senator Wharton and whoever is working with him."

"What should I do?" I whispered, suddenly shivering despite the unseasonably warm weather.

He dropped his hands from my arms. "You know how bad Senator Wharton wants to be president. Be very careful. Don't trust anyone. Keep your eyes open, and your mouth shut." He glanced over his shoulder for the hundredth time. "I have to go."

"Why are you helping me?"

A faint smile lifted the corners of his lips. "Because you're a good person. Because I shouldn't have left my iPad where you could pick it up. I feel responsible." He brushed my hair from my face. "I'm sorry."

He pivoted on his heel and walked away. I dropped my head into my hands. I didn't know if I could do this. I wanted to run away and start a new life far away from all this shit. I felt sorry for those women, but what could I do?

As I stood at the edge of the Reflection Pool, I didn't recognize the reflection staring back at me. I ached with bone-deep betrayal, and my mind had divorced itself from my body. I would've never believed my stepdad could so effortlessly turn on me, but I misjudged him. I didn't know him at all.

By the time I reached my car, my entire body shook from the sudden weather change and the conversation with Brandon. I dropped my key fob when I pulled it out of my pocket. Bending down, I noticed my front driver's side tire was flat.

Shocked, I ran my finger along the outside of the tire looking for a nail when I noticed a one-inch slash in the sidewall. There was no way I could change a tire by myself. It was starting to drizzle, and I didn't know how to do it anyway.

I called a tow truck and Winnie, and then I slid into the front seat of my car to wait. A white piece of paper tucked under the windshield wiper of my car caught my attention. I rolled down the window and snagged it. I unfolded it and saw a typewritten note in all caps.

STAY AWAY FROM ARCHER BLACK.
HE CAN'T BE TRUSTED.

Stunned, the note slipped from my fingertips into the passenger seat of my car. I didn't know if the note was a threat or a warning. Brandon warned me not to trust anyone, but he told me in person. The note wasn't from him. That left my stepdad or someone else who didn't want me around Archer, like an ex-girlfriend.

I averted my gaze from the note, staring out the window. The sender's identity wasn't relevant. I had been so careful to maintain control over my life since I broke up with Brandon, but now everything was spiraling away faster than I could've imagined possible.

CHAPTER SEVENTEEN

Archer

I settled into a small black chair in the waiting area of Langley's work. It had been three days since we had talked and six days since I had seen her. Knox didn't have any information about her meeting with Brandon other than a confirmation that it happened. Knox's investigator couldn't get close enough to the conversation to hear any details, but he commented that Brandon looked nervous the entire time, glancing over his shoulder often and rubbing his hands together. Since her meeting, Langley had done everything she could to avoid me, which put me on edge in more ways than one.

The quick search of her home didn't reveal anything new either, but that wasn't surprising. Knox didn't dig for anything not in plain sight, and Langley wouldn't have left any personal details in the open anyway. The only information Knox gleaned from the brief search was a confirmation that Senator Wharton's surveillance extended to the inside of her home in addition to the loose tail he had on her day-to-day movements.

I studied her as she finally finished with her last client before her lunch break. Every other time I'd seen her see was dressed up, but today she wore black yoga pants and a light blue t-shirt. Her golden blonde hair was in a thick, loose braid that dangled between her shoulder blades with every movement.

Just like every other time I saw her, a heavy dose of lust and possessiveness slammed into me. Now that I had touched her, kissed her, and caressed every curve of her body, the feeling nearly overwhelmed me. She distracted me from my goal.

I clutched the arms of the chair when our gazes clashed. She retreated a few steps, and I stood up, refusing to let her push me away for one more minute. This dance she'd been playing since she walked out my door on Saturday afternoon had to end.

"Langley."

She shot me a questioning look. "Archer, what are you doing here?"

I took a step forward and she took a step back. "You're avoiding me."

She shook her head, and a delicate flush stained her lustrous skin. "No, I'm not."

"Do you really expect me to believe that?"

"I don't know why you wouldn't. I've been swamped with work." Her eyes darted around the gym. One of her male co-workers watched us as his patient yanked on a red exercise band tied to a silver metal chin-up bar.

"So swamped that you can't answer my calls?"

"Archer, I can't talk here. Maybe we can meet after work."

I snatched her hand and threaded my fingers through hers. "Isn't it time for your lunch break?"

"Yes, but I have paperwork and a few calls to make." She tried and failed to slip her hand from my grasp.

"Forget the paperwork. We need to talk."

"Langley, is everything all right?" her co-worker questioned as he strolled forward to join the conversation.

Langley smiled politely, but it didn't reach her eyes. "I'm fine, Todd." She gestured to me. "This is Archer, a friend of mine."

Todd looked back and forth between Langley and me. I didn't miss the way his eyes lingered on her body. He wanted her. Well, too bad. It wouldn't happen. For the time being, Langley belonged to me.

"Okay. Did you still want to go to lunch in ten minutes?" Todd asked.

My eyes snapped to Langley's face, and I gritted my teeth. A foreign surge of jealousy knocked me off balance. I couldn't recall being jealous over a woman before. Either they were faithful to me while we dated, or I severed ties and never looked back. I didn't care enough to attach any emotion to a relationship. I enjoyed it while it lasted, and when the chemistry fizzled, I ended the connection without much thought. Relationships were secondary to my career goals. It had always been that way, and it pissed me off that Langley made me feel any different.

"Can we do it tomorrow instead?" she said, ignoring my heated glare.

"Sure. I'll be here." Todd squeezed her shoulder and returned to his patient.

"Looks like we're going to lunch. Do you want to grab your purse or are you ready to go?"

"As long as you're paying we can go. I only have thirty minutes, though."

"That should be enough time." I wrapped my arm around her waist and guided her out the door. The gesture wasn't necessary, but I wanted Todd to know Langley and I were more than friends.

As I instructed, my car service waited right outside the door. I opened the door and gestured for her to get in the car. Silence greeted me when I slid in the backseat next to Langley. Like a barnacle on the bottom of a boat, she pressed her body against the opposite door and stared out the window.

After sixty seconds, I'd had enough. Langley owed me an explanation. She had been avoiding me since Saturday morning, and she still hadn't mentioned her meeting with Brandon. With a press of a button, I raised the retractable privacy window.

"So now we're friends? That's it?" I said sharply, drumming my fingers impatiently on my thigh.

"Yes, we're friends." She didn't bother to glance at me as she responded.

"Can you clarify something for me?"

Her fingers nervously fretting with a thread dangling from the hem of her shirt, she finally met my gaze. "Yes?"

"Were we just friends on Friday night, or were

we something more and you've since decided you're not interested in me?"

Twisting the end of her thick braid, she blew out an exaggerated breath. "Archer, I like you. I really do. We had a good time on Friday, but I can't be in a relationship right now. It won't work."

I slid across the seat so my leg pressed against hers. "That's it? It's over just like that," I said quietly. Disappointment settled in my gut like a lead ball. I shouldn't let her affect me like this. It was ridiculous, inconvenient, and a bad idea, but I couldn't stop it.

She stared at the center of my chest, suddenly unwilling to meet my eyes. "Yes, it's over. It's nothing personal, okay? There are a lot of things going on in my life, and I don't want to drag you into this mess."

"Damn it, Langley." I tipped up her chin, being careful not to hurt her. "Look at me."

Her eyes flickered to mine and then dropped to my chest again. "I'm sorry. I'm not good at this."

"What part? The talking or the dumping?"

"Either. Both. I don't know."

"Ah," I responded, dropping my hand from her face. The muscle in my jaw flexed with anger, but I kept my voice calm...almost mild. "Does this have anything to do with your meeting with Brandon on Saturday? Are you back together with him now? Is that what this is about?"

She held up her hand. "Archer, I—"

"Don't spout pretty platitudes. Tell me the truth. I think I deserve that. Don't you?"

Wide-eyed, she stared at me, not saying a single

word. Then, she shook her head. "Yes, but it isn't that simple."

"Give it a try."

"This…" she waved her hand back and forth between us. "Doesn't have anything to do with Brandon. I don't want anything to do with him. I hate him. I regret that I was involved with him, and I don't repeat my mistakes."

I slammed my hand against the back of the seat. "Then why did you sneak away from my house on Saturday to meet him?"

"How did you know?"

The question surprised me, and my muscles tensed. Seconds ticked by as I tried to come up with a reasonable explanation. In the end, I decided to tell her the truth. "I overheard you talking on the phone."

She sighed. "I didn't sneak anywhere. You had a meeting, remember?"

"But you met him. Why?"

"It's none of your business, but we had something to discuss. Stop interrogating me."

"You're my girlfriend. Of course it's my business when you meet with your ex after you climb out of my bed."

"Fuck you!" She shoved my chest, but I didn't budge. "I'm not your girlfriend."

"That's where you're wrong." In one seamless maneuver, I lifted her and placed her on my lap. Her pupils dilated, then her lashes fluttered as her pulse throbbed at the hollow of her neck, confirming our hunger for each other wasn't one-sided.

Time suspended as lust simmered between us. I

wanted her, and not because of Senator Wharton or anything else. I just wanted her. I captured her lips in a hard kiss. For one drawn out second, her mouth didn't move, but she didn't fight me either. Every muscle in her body tightened, her potential rejection hovered like a specter, taunting me.

Then, she nipped my lower lip, and brushed her lips against mine, almost like an apology. "This is bad," she muttered against my lips, even as she pressed her body closer to mine. "This isn't a good decision for either of us. We shouldn't do this."

"You're wrong." I licked the seam of her lips, demanding access, and she complied. Our tongues danced, and with every swirl, her denial of us and rejection of me faded as though it never happened. I adjusted her legs so that she straddled my waist, shifting our bodies closer together. Heat slammed into me, fast and hard. The timing sucked, but I had to be inside her again.

"But the driver. We can't do this here. Now. Are you crazy?"

"He won't bother us." I pulled her closer, rubbing her against the ridge in my pants, telling her without words how much I wanted her. How much I missed her. How much I needed her even though I shouldn't feel any of those things. It was wrong. Everything about wanting Langley like this was wrong, but damn, it felt right.

With every call and text she dodged over the last four days, I felt angry.

Angry that I noticed.

Angry that I cared.

Angry that this woman elicited such strong

emotions from me.

I could blame it on bad timing or a sick twist of destiny. It didn't matter either way because I couldn't deny it.

"Archer," she moaned, circling her arms around my neck, pulling me closer like I was her anchor. She moved her hips against me restlessly. Each artless arch and circle of her hips drove me wild until fiery lust burned through my veins demanding her complete surrender.

"I know." I cupped her ass and squeezed, not hard enough to hurt, but hard enough to let her know this was my game. I was in control. "By the way, did I mention how good you look in your work attire?" I rolled my hips. Her eyes fluttered, and her back bowed in invitation.

She rolled her head from side to side. "This feels so good. Too good. You're killing me. You know that, right?"

"How? Tell me," I demanded as my lips trailed down the side of her neck. Kissing her. Tasting her. Licking her. Claiming her. She tasted and smelled like my personal addiction in the making. A little sweet. A little salty. More than a little perfect.

"Because I want you, but I can't have you. Not now. Maybe never," she said, her voice pained and her eyes glistening. "But I can't stop myself."

She tugged at the bottom of my shirt, releasing it from my pants, and her hands whispered over my chest and my stomach. My muscles jumped under the silky-smooth pads of her fingertips, begging for more. Every touch was like torture.

Torture because I wanted more.

Torture because Langley was the wrong woman to want like this.

Torture because we were enemies, even if she didn't know it yet.

Torture because we couldn't be together once I revealed the truth.

Torture because I was utterly fucked.

"You have me," I confided, even though I realized those three were a lie. If I could alter reality and make my connection to Senator Wharton disappear, I would in a heartbeat.

"Prove it," she whispered, releasing my belt buckle and freeing my cock.

Her words raced down my spine, making my dick harder than I thought possible. She didn't have to repeat her request. I yanked her pants down her legs, freeing one leg and not bothering with the other.

My hands raked over her exposed golden-kissed skin. She really was a beautiful woman—maybe the most beautiful woman I'd ever touched.

She nipped my earlobe. "I want you inside of me."

Shit. I nearly exploded from her simple but direct demand. She was too tempting when she looked at me with her lips damp from my kisses. "Take what you want," I said, my voice husky even though I knew I should stop this right now, but I couldn't. My muscles were strung tight like a rubber band ready to snap.

Her lustrous green eyes never left mine as she lowered her body, taking me inside of her one inch at a time. Once fully seated, her eyes drifted closed and I nearly growled at the perfection in front of me. She looked angelic with the muted sunlight from the tinted windows dancing through her golden hair, her long dark lashes fanning her elegantly sculpted cheekbones, and her sultry lips parted. I leaned forward and brushed a kiss against her swollen lips as I twisted the length of her braid around my hand.

As much as part of me wanted to revel in the moment, savor our connection, and get drunk on her beauty, I couldn't. I was too far gone. With every passing second, my control fractured a little more. Not that I would complain. Since she walked out of my door on Saturday, I had been obsessed with getting her back in my bed, and even though this wasn't my bed, it'd work. For now.

Gripping her waist, I rocked my hips into her, and she started to move.

Up.

Down.

Up.

Down.

Wanting control, I flipped her onto her back, and I slammed into her over and over, grinding against her pelvis, taking what I wanted and giving her what she needed. With every thrust, I slipped into a place I shouldn't go, especially not with her. But my brain was too fuzzy with lust to do anything about it. There were no more thoughts of revenge or destroying Senator Wharton. Only us. Only this moment. It was unequaled and untainted.

Her sharp inhalation followed by a shaky moan, echoed through the car like music to my ears. The prison bars around my heart rattled and warped and somehow Langley swept inside like she'd always belonged there. This wasn't going to last long, but I didn't care, and I didn't think she did either.

Tilting her hips up, I deepened my thrusts. Pleasure zipped through my body making me greedy for her. "Do you still think we should end this?" I groaned next to her ear. "Is that what you really want?"

"No," she whispered, the single word tangling with a throaty moan.

"Remember that the next time you try to throw us away." My voice was thick with lust, need, and a little desperation. I was only distantly aware that we were still in my car, my driver not five feet away with only a sheet of glass separating him from us.

Her eyes opened, holding my gaze. A sensual smile toyed with the corner of her lips. "Yes," she murmured, tracing the angle of my jaw with her fingertips.

That simple word combined with the sultry glow of her eyes ignited a soul-stealing tremor down my spine. My willpower splintered as I moved frantically in and out of her, chasing our mutual release like this could be our last.

"Fuck," I half-groaned, half-growled as a warm fervor rushed through my blood like a shot of morphine.

Then, she screamed, and I devoured her erotic cries with my mouth. Our breath mingled. Our tongues knitted together like two pieces of a puzzle, and I continued moving and taking what I wanted. With every flex of my hips, her inner muscles clenched around me, robbing me of coherent thought. Even if I wanted to hold back, I didn't think I'd succeed, so I let go.

Like being hit by wrecking ball, a seismic wave of pleasure ripped through my body, and I spilled inside her. Our eyes locked in an embrace, and we rode every swell of mutual euphoria, hard and fast, until everything but the two of us joined together in bliss, vanished from memory.

With unfocused eyes, she stared up at me, her thick, golden braid spilling off the leather seat and swinging back and forth like a pendulum. Leaning forward, I brushed a kiss over her lips.

Slowly, I untangled our bodies. I watched as she pulled up her pants and smoothed her hair. Then, I zipped and buckled my pants. The backseat of the car suddenly felt too small as I waited for her to say something…anything.

Did she regret it? Did she think I pressured her? Fuck. I didn't want her to push me away, even though it'd probably be the best outcome for both of us. Eventually, I'd ruin her with my quest for revenge, and her inevitable rejection of me would cut deeper than I wanted to admit. Maybe it had something to do with being rejected by my father. I didn't want to analyze it, but I couldn't ignore it either.

"I guess I don't have time for lunch now," she said and then laughed. Her laugh was like an arrow piercing my heart, claiming me before I had the wherewithal to object.

"We can stop somewhere and grab something quick."

"I can't." She tapped the rectangular face of my wristwatch. "I have a patient in ten minutes."

"Cancel it," I said, even though I knew she couldn't.

"I can't."

"Okay. I'll bring you some food after I drop you off."

"You don't have to do that."

I tugged on the end of her braid. "I know, but I want to. What kind of lunch date would I be if I sent you back to work hungry?"

She smiled. "A very satisfying one."

I chuckled. "Don't start or you will have to cancel you next appointment."

"I wish we could spend the afternoon together," she said, the smile slipping off her face.

She opened the car door to get out.

"Wait." I grabbed her wrist.

"What?"

"We still need to talk. Can I meet you at your house tonight at six? Will that work?"

"No." Her eyes darted toward the entrance of her work. "I'll come over to your place."

"All right. I'll see you at six."

She nodded. "Six," she said, then stepped out of the car without another word.

Damn her. Something was definitely going on with her, and she didn't have any intention of sharing it with me. I'd be pissed if I weren't so fascinated by her.

CHAPTER EIGHTEEN

Langley

The rest of my day was awful. I couldn't concentrate on my patients. Guilt twisted my stomach into a pretzel for failing to sever ties with Archer. Todd's eyes followed me all afternoon as though he suspected how I'd spent my lunch break.

My emotions fluctuated wildly. One second, I was drowning in shame because I'd succumbed to Archer's skillful seduction. The next, an overwhelming anxiety threatened to swallow me whole. My mind jogged in circles as I analyzed the pros and cons of being with Archer or giving him up.

Around four in the afternoon, as I watched my patient do a set of hip rotation exercises, I realized I couldn't see Archer again unless I escaped my stepdad's range of influence.

The first day after meeting Brandon, I'd convinced myself the accusations against my stepdad were crazy. The second day, I started to believe they held some truth. The third day, devastation settled into my heart. The last three days, I started questioning Archer's suspiciously timed arrival in my life. I didn't know what to believe anymore, and I guess it was irrelevant. Regardless of his motives, I didn't have room for Archer in my life right now.

What did I really know about Archer besides what I'd read in the newspapers? He only allowed me to see what he wanted me to see—a carefully crafted illusion of a successful and considerate man in a five thousand dollar suit. The core of the real man behind the financial wizard with a compelling rags to riches story was unavailable, and I didn't think he had any intention of inviting me inside anytime in the near future.

I'd spent my entire life in the clutches of the Wharton political machine where smoke and mirrors were the norm, not the exception, so I knew a façade when I saw one, and Archer had a good one. Unfortunately, with his little gestures— defending me from Brandon, accompanying me home, flowers, lunches—he'd sailed through my defenses, which meant I needed to end things permanently this time. Preferably before he had forged a lasting place in my heart.

When my last patient left at five thirty, I ran out the door without bothering to do paperwork. I paused as I reached the side of my car. Just like last weekend after I'd met with Brandon, a white piece of paper was stuffed under my windshield wiper. With trembling hands, I snatched the folded piece of paper off my windshield and got into the car.

For long seconds, I didn't do anything. I stared at the paper in my lap. Part of me wanted to crumble it into a ball and toss it out the window without reading it, but in the end I opened the note. I didn't have a choice.

Stay away from Archer Black.
This is your last warning.

My gut twisted into knots, and a whimper escaped my mouth. I cupped my face with my hands as silent tears tracked down my face. This was so fucked up. I couldn't do this anymore. I didn't know where to turn. I didn't know who to trust. The only person who I still had faith in was Winnie, and there was no way I'd willingly drag her into this.

Unable to navigate the riddle my life had become, I tucked the note into my glove box and started driving. Instead of going to Archer's house as I promised, I drove home. The minute I walked through my front door, I didn't make the effort to change my clothes. I snagged a bottle of wine and a wine glass and turned on the television.

Two glasses of wine and thirty minutes after the designated time to go over Archer's house, I sent him a text.

Me: Something came up. I can't meet tonight.

Archer responded almost immediately.

Archer: Can I pick you up for breakfast

tomorrow morning?

I dropped my phone on the coffee table, and my nails dug into my clenched fists. I didn't know how to respond. As much as I wanted to crawl into Archer's bed, find shelter in his arms, and forget all my problems, I wouldn't let myself succumb to the desire to be close to him. I knew I'd regret it, but I had to let him go. I couldn't trust him and couldn't involve him in my messy life. Not now. Maybe never.

For the first time in my life, I was tempted to end a relationship over a text message. Just like this afternoon, I had no doubt Archer would skillfully evade my attempts to sever our relationship if I met him in person. After composing and deleting no less than five breakup texts, my mature side persevered. I was twenty-four, not sixteen. Twenty-four-year-olds didn't dump someone by text. Well, they did, but I refused to do it. Instead, I composed a text aimed at buying time before I had to see him again.

Me: I have plans tomorrow.

For the most part, the text was the truth. Tomorrow morning, like most Saturday mornings, I had plans to play tennis with my mom. As much as I didn't want to see my mom or stepdad, canceling would raise suspicion.

An hour passed and Archer hadn't responded, which disappointed me more than I wanted to acknowledge. After habitually checking my phone for the next half hour, I turned it off and stuffed my phone under the sofa cushion. I mentally slapped myself for caring or believing Archer wouldn't give up...that he wanted me enough to keep fighting for us.

Archer probably had a long list of women on speed dial, breathlessly waiting for him to invite them to do anything no matter how small or inconsequential. He was the whole package—wealthy, sinfully attractive, smart, and successful. I don't know why I believed he'd continue to pursue me after I had pushed him away time and time again. It didn't make sense.

I shook my head, chiding myself for losing focus. As far as I knew, I was the woman of the month, nothing more. I needed to stop romanticizing what had happened between us over the last few weeks and get over it. There was a reason why I stayed far away from men like Archer. He made me want too much. Need too much. Care too much.

More important issues required my attention...like my stepdad monitoring my calls and my home, the threatening notes on my car, and the colossal scandal brewing around my family. If my stepdad weren't such a narcissist, he'd drop his plans to run for president.

Just as I drifted off to sleep, someone banged on my door, and I bolted upright on the sofa, knocking over my glass of wine in the process. *Shit.* Instead of heading for the door, I snagged a roll of paper towels off the counter to blot the pink hue of the rosé wine from my cream and gray prism wool rug.

The banging started again, harder and longer this

time, rattling the frame of my aged wood door. "Who is it?" I yelled, still on my hands and knees next to the sofa.

"It's Archer. Open the door, Langley."

I crushed the paper towel into a tight ball. I couldn't let him come in my house for so many reasons, not the least of which was the listening devices that may or may not be hidden somewhere in my house. For all I knew, there could be cameras too. I shivered thinking of the invisible eyes crawling all over me, inspecting and cataloging every move.

"What are you doing here?"

"I want to talk."

I tossed the damp paper towel on my coffee table and cautiously shuffled to my door. "Now's not a good time. Maybe later."

"Dammit, Langley. What the hell is going on?"

I rested my head against the door, unable and unwilling to answer his question. I didn't know where to start, which made me feel more alone than I had in recent memory. "I'm sorry, Archer. I can't explain."

He slammed his hand against the door, and the heavy wood rattled in the doorjamb. "Langley, are you serious? Open the door."

I paced in front of door like a madwoman contemplating my options. I didn't have any. "Fine," I groaned. My hands shaking, I fumbled with the lock and then swung the door open.

Not waiting for an invitation, he stalked into my house. His dark eyebrows slashed downward, and his inky hair stuck up as though he'd ran his hand through it a hundred times in the last hour. He stared down at me for a long beat without saying a word, and my heart hammered in my chest awaiting what? His judgment. His next move. His final dismissal. I didn't know.

"Why are you doing this?" He took one long stride toward me, his nearly black eyes glittering with a predatory gleam. "After what happened in the car today, I thought we were on the same page, but now we're right back where we started before lunch," he said harshly as he scrubbed his hand along the faint stubble on his jaw. "Just because you're waffling right now doesn't mean I'll back off, Langley…not by a long shot."

"You don't have a choice. I tried to tell you today before you distracted me."

"You tried to tell me what?"

I yanked his arm, dragging him out of my house and onto the front stoop. I slammed the door behind us. "I can't sleep with you again. What happened today was wrong. You shouldn't be here." Despite my well-intentioned words, my mind wavered as the low hum of arousal buzzed through my body, lapping up his presence like it'd been a month since I'd seen him instead of hours. How did he do this to me?

"Wrong? How?" His eyes flickered to my closed door and then scanned my face. "Is there someone here with you?"

"No." I positioned my body between the front door and him. I couldn't let him go inside.

He looped his arm around my waist and caught his bottom lip between his teeth and then released it slowly as he leaned forward. I swayed into him like a blade of grass in the wind, helpless to stop myself. His dark hooded eyes worked better than a master hypnotist. I was under his spell, my lips already tingling in covetous expectancy of his kiss.

"Then you won't mind if I look around," he whispered, his warm minty breath caressing my face. The door flung open behind me, and he darted around me.

Damn him. "Get out." I wrapped my arms around his waist, pressing my chest against the hard planes of his back. If Brandon's accusations were accurate, I didn't need my stepdad getting an earful or eyeful of Archer and whatever he had to say. "Please. Let's not do this here," I begged. Desperation clawed at my chest.

His muscles tensed under my fingertips. Then, he broke my hold on his waist and whirled around to face me in one smooth movement. His eyes flared with irritation and something else I didn't recognize. "Why not here?"

"I can't explain," I said almost soundlessly, hoping my voice was too low for any listening device. God, I felt like I was going to explode under the weight of all the paranoia that had taken up a permanent residence in my mind since the meeting with Brandon.

"Name the time and place and stick to it," he bit out. "Because I don't like this cat and mouse game you're playing with me."

I shook my head slowly, keeping my eyes fastened on his. "I'm not playing with you."

"How would you explain what you're doing?"

"Complicated."

"Then, uncomplicate it or explain it." His voice was like gravel on glass. His muscles were coiled and the vein in his neck pulsed. I cringed at the frustration and anger rolling off him in waves.

I scanned the interior of my home, taking in the gray sofa, the painstakingly restored hardwood floor planks, and the photographs of friends and family lining the fireplace mantle. It didn't even feel like my home anymore. In every detail, I saw a potential invasion of my privacy, and violated didn't begin to describe the emotion burning like gasoline through my veins.

Every time I tried to push my stepdad away, some event, comment, or circumstance snapped me back into his sphere of influence. I didn't know why my mom married him or stayed with him. I hated him. I hated what he'd done to my life, my mom, and my future. I hated his phony speeches feigning compassion for the less fortunate members of society. Senator Wharton only cared about himself and how fast he could climb the political ladders of power. Whose back he stepped on to get there didn't matter. They were collateral damage sacrificed to nourish his delusions of grandeur and glory.

I may not be able to trust Archer, but I sure as hell couldn't trust my stepdad. He was a liar, and he could be a murderer, which meant I was done.

Done protecting him and his political legacy.

Done playing the perfect family.

Done putting my life on hold for him and my mom.

Done sacrificing myself at the altar of the Wharton political machine.

I yanked my purse and gym bag off the hook in my entryway. I needed to get out of my house. Like everything else in my life, it belonged to Senator Wharton. I didn't want to take the time to pack. His people could spy on this place all they wanted because I wouldn't be here. Not anymore. I'd petition the trustee of the trust my dad left me for additional funds if I had to. I didn't care.

"Let's go to your house." The rawness in my voice made me flinch. I didn't realize how close I was to crying. I took a few deep breaths to regain my equilibrium and suppress the urge to collapse into a chasm of despair and self-pity.

"Langley…" He paused and sucked in a huge breath. "Are you okay? Do you want to talk about it?"

"I'll tell you everything when we get to your house," I said, massaging my temples. My head literally ached from the mental stress of the last week.

The meeting with Brandon.

The notes on my car.

The invasion of my privacy.

I couldn't do this anymore. I needed help.

CHAPTER NINETEEN

Archer

Langley stood in front of the floor-to-ceiling windows overlooking the Potomac. I always liked the view. It was one of the reasons I bought the place. At night, the way the yellow lights of the buildings danced on the water's surface took my breath away, but watching Langley with her golden hair flowing down her back literally made my heart clench. Lost in her thoughts and as still as a statue, she looked tragically beautiful.

"Do you want a glass of wine?" I asked.

"Sure," she said absently. I wondered if she even heard me.

"Is red okay?"

"It's fine. I don't normally drink red. I love it, but it gives me a headache."

I paused with the corkscrew halfway into the cork. "Are you sure? I can open something else. I have a chardonnay and a rosé too."

"No, tonight I feel like red." She nodded and

then cleared her throat. "I have reason to believe my stepdad is monitoring my phone calls," Langley said, not bothering to look at me when she dropped that bomb.

I froze mid-pour. Two drops of burgundy-colored wine splashed in the wineglass. That wasn't the direction I anticipated this discussion going. Truthfully, I didn't know exactly why she wanted to terminate our relationship, but I suspected it had something to do with pressure from Senator Wharton and his campaign advisors. On the face, Senator Wharton's opposition to me didn't make sense, but who knows what kind of lies he fed her.

Carrying two glasses of wine, I crossed the room. "Why do you think that?"

She wrapped her arms around her torso. "Brandon told me last weekend."

"And you believe him?"

She turned around, facing me for the first time since we walked in my home. Her normally golden skin was pale, and her normally vibrant eyes looked empty. I handed her the glass of wine. She took it and walked to the sofa and sat.

"Not at first. It seemed crazy." She shook her head as she stared at the wall. "But now..." Her voice faded to nothing, and I didn't think she'd finished her thought. She twirled the wineglass in her hand by the stem. "But now, I think he's right."

I eyed her carefully, not wanting to give anything away. She was right, or at least according to Knox's sources. "Why?"

"It makes sense."

"Ah." I sat down next to her on the sofa. "How

so?"

She took a drink of her wine, then placed it on the coffee table. Rubbing her hands along her thighs, she stared at the far wall before she shifted to face me. "Can I trust you? I mean really trust you, because I don't have anyone to help me. I don't trust Brandon. My mom will choose *him* over me, and I don't want to involve Winnie in something like this. I know we haven't known each other long, but I don't know where to turn. I'm a little out of my depth here."

"Yes," I said, placing my hand on her leg. At that second, with her red-rimmed eyes and vulnerable gaze, I promised myself if I could find a way to protect both of us, I would do it. Destroying Senator Wharton didn't mean I had to destroy her too.

Her green eyes searched mine, and after a few seconds, she inclined her head. "Okay. I don't know where to start."

"Start at the beginning." I needed to know everything.

She leaned back against the chair. "I saw an email to Brandon from my stepdad. He wanted Brandon to convince ten women to sign a nondisclosure agreement. Apparently, he had a relationship with these women, and he didn't want them to sell their stories. I didn't finish reading it, but to make a long story short, I knew I couldn't be with Brandon anymore. We agreed to go our separate ways, and I agreed not to confront Senator Wharton or reveal any of the details to my mom."

"Why did you agree to keep the secret?"

"Honestly, I don't know. At the time, it made

sense, and it kept me out of my stepdad's life." She ran her hands through her hair. "I can't give a good reason other than I acted in my self-interest. I didn't want to be involved."

"So you think Senator Wharton is watching you because of that email?" It seemed like a stretch. There had to be more to the story. Senator Wharton was watching her. I knew that, but I'd always thought there would be more to the story than a string of affairs.

"Three of the ten women are dead. The same three women who refused to sign the nondisclosure agreement. All ten women were underage escorts at the time of the affair, and according to Brandon, all of the ten women are connected to Gerald Whittaker. The same Gerald Whittaker who was arrested recently."

"Fuck," I said, standing up. I circled the coffee table like a caged tiger as my world tilted upside down and inside out. Everything I suspected was true. "Did Senator Wharton kill those women?" Every instinct in my gut screamed for blood. I didn't want revenge anymore. I wanted Senator Wharton to rot in hell, and not just for what he'd done to my family and me but for tearing apart Langley's life too.

"Brandon implied as much, but all three deaths were ruled a suicide."

"Fucking hell." I bent at my waist, unable to calm the blood pumping wildly through my veins. I heard the rumors about Gerald Whittaker. It didn't take long for me to piece Senator Wharton's web of lies and depravity together.

"Is it too much?" she asked almost soundlessly as she smeared the condensation on her wine glass with her fingertip. "Do you want to run away from me? I'd like to run away from myself. I can't believe I didn't do anything six months ago." She downed the rest of her wine and stood up. She walked toward the door. "I know it's a lot to ask, but I'd appreciate if you kept this information quiet...at least for a little while."

"Where are you going?" I asked when her hand circled for the doorknob.

"I don't know. I'll get a hotel tonight." She shrugged, gripping the doorknob so hard her knuckles whitened. "Then, who knows? My dad has a sister. I haven't seen or heard from her since my dad's death, but I might try to find her. I think she still lives in California. Maybe she'll help me," she said with an air of finality and fierce determination.

"You're not leaving."

"I'm not?" She turned on her heel and pressed her back against the door.

"No." I crossed the room in seconds, wrapping my arms around her and pulling her into my embrace. I stroked the back of her hair with my hand. "I'm going to help you. We'll figure this out together."

"How?" she whispered into my chest. "What can you do?"

"Other than Brandon's story, do you have any evidence to support these allegations?"

Her muscles tensed under my hands, and she drew a few shallow breaths into her lungs. She lifted her chin, and her eyes swam with unshed tears. "I printed the email between Brandon and my stepdad. It lists the women's names and addresses."

"Where is it?"

"At my house."

"Okay." My chest heaved and grief for my mother rolled in my gut. "We need to get it and put it somewhere safe." With a blinding clarity, I knew I had every piece of evidence I needed to destroy Senator Wharton. I could link him to those women with his own words, and with a little digging around, I could pin the deaths of those three women on him.

"How?" She shivered. "I don't want to go back there ever again. He has listening devices in my home. I haven't found them, but I'm sure of it. That's why I didn't want to talk to you there tonight."

"Can you tell me exactly where you hid the email?"

She rubbed her eyes. "Yes."

"I'll take care of everything." And I would...no matter what.

CHAPTER TWENTY

Langley

For the last hour, I couldn't sit down. I had paced the length of Archer's living room at least a hundred times as my emotions seesawed up and down. Desperate to empty my mind of the worries ruling my thoughts, I tried to think about other things—the tennis match with my mom tomorrow, Winnie's invitation to brunch on Sunday, my hair appointment on Monday during my lunch break.

After Archer had cooked me a simple dinner, he retreated to his study to make some phone calls. I should have joined him and participated in whatever he was planning, but I couldn't face reality yet. I had revealed enough dirt to destroy my stepdad, and I had offered him the supporting evidence on a platter. That was enough for one day.

Relief and bone-deep sadness ate at my gut. Relief that Archer agreed to help me, and sadness that I had pulled the trigger of the gun that would destroy the only family I had for the last twelve years. My mom wasn't the type of mother I would've picked if I had the choice, but she was still my mother. I didn't want to hurt her, but I didn't have a choice anymore. If my stepdad had anything to do with murdering those three women, I couldn't blindly trust he wouldn't do the same to me.

I didn't know why Archer agreed to help me. It didn't make sense, but there was no going back now. For better or worse, I had made the decision to include him. Now I had to wait and see what happened. We were in this together.

A key turned in the front door of Archer's home, and bile rose up in my dry throat. This was it. Something was going to happen. Turning back was no longer an option. I was going to throw up.

"Relax, Langley," Archer whispered next to my ear as he twined his arm around my waist. "It's just my brother, Knox. I sent him to your house to get the letter and pack you a bag."

"Can we trust him?" I asked, staring at the sharp angles of Archer's profile.

"You can trust me," Knox said. A huge grin split across his face as he stepped into Archer's house and closed the door behind him, taking time to secure the deadbolt.

Knox didn't look anything like Archer. Knox had shaggy blonde hair and light, almost transparent, eyes. Where Archer was brooding and intense, Knox seemed free-spirited and light, right down to his casual clothes and easy smile.

"You don't look like brothers," I commented as I scanned the two of them, looking for similarities.

"We have different fathers," Archer answered without glancing at me. "Let's talk in the study."

Five minutes later, we were all seated in the chairs flanking Archer's desk. My hands trembled as I gripped the wooden arms of my seat.

"Did you find the letter?" Archer questioned, directing his hardened gaze at Knox.

Knox's gaze flickered to me before returning to Archer. "It was exactly where you said it would be."

"Good. Can I see it?"

Knox pulled a paper folded in fours from a gray canvas messenger bag and handed it to Archer. My heart skipped a beat when I recognized the paper I'd been hiding for over six months.

With his mouth pressed into a rigid line, Archer scanned the email. "Have you read this?" he asked Knox.

"I did," Knox confirmed, his eyes narrowing fractionally before his face smoothed into a blank mask once again. "And I made copies."

"Why do you need copies?" I shifted in my seat to face Knox. I confided in Archer, and apparently by default, Knox, but I didn't know anything about him.

"For my investigation."

"Your what?" Glaring at Archer, I stood up and folded my arms across my chest. "I shared this information with you, but that didn't mean I agreed to let you make the next call. This is my life." I held out my open palm and wiggled my fingers. "I want the email back along with all the copies. If I need your help, I'll ask. Until then, back off."

"No." Archer leaned forward, bracing his elbows on the edge of the desk.

"No?" I echoed, my eyebrows scaling my forehead in disbelief.

"You can't do this alone." Archer jumped out of his chair. He stalked around the side of his desk, only stopping when he stood in front of me.

"If I don't do anything and he's elected, maybe he'll leave me alone. He won't care about me anymore." Even as the words tumbled from my mouth, I didn't believe them. I couldn't see any way out of this mess, but that realization didn't stop me from second guessing my next move.

"And you're happy with that result?" Archer challenged, his dark eyes flashing with anger. "Happy with a man who might have arranged the murder of three women becoming the next President of the United States?"

"I doubt it would be the first time or the last time an unethical person is elected to a higher office." I cringed as I said the words, because I didn't want my stepdad to succeed, but the statement was the truth. The little I had learned about politics over the last decade taught me there wasn't a place for lofty ideals and morals inside the Beltway.

"Langley," Knox said, interrupting the standoff between Archer and me. "Whether Senator Wharton is elected is irrelevant. In his mind, you have the power to destroy him. Don't kid yourself. He will do what's necessary to neutralize that threat. It might happen next week, or it might happen two years from now. You can't sit around playing defense, waiting for him to make his first move.

You need to play offense and catch him off guard."

"Are you implying he might kill me?" Tears burned the corners of my eyes. Fuck. I blinked repeatedly, trying to quell the urge to cry. I hated being weak. I wished I could press the pause button on my life for a few months while I figured out what to do.

Knox shrugged. "You know him better than I do, but don't you think you're a little too old to pretend you can close your eyes, click your heels three times, and everything will disappear?"

His words were like a knife picking at an old wound. I had closed my eyes and looked the other way when it came to my stepdad too many times to count. The email wasn't my first clue Senator Wharton wasn't who he pretended to be in front of the cameras. "Who are you to judge me?"

Archer pulled me into an embrace and wiped the tears streaming down my face with the pads of his fingers. "Listen to what Knox is saying," he whispered next my ear. "He knows what he's doing. He worked as a naval intelligence officer. He can help you. We both can. Give us the chance to help you."

"I don't know if I can do this. You don't understand." I shook my head. "People owe him favors. He can make the allegations disappear. What I say won't matter. I've seen him do it before. The Wharton political machine will systematically assassinate my character and somehow paint my stepdad as a sympathetic character in the process." I stepped out of Archer's hold. "That's what they do. White is black and black is white to them. Only winning matters, not facts."

"Exactly. Except this time we're going to win."

I swallowed hard, working to lubricate my sudden dry throat. "You don't know what you're talking about."

Archer's lips curled at the corners, forming something resembling a sinister smile. "That's where you're wrong. Senator Wharton has money and power, but so do I, and I have no intention of losing this fight."

I eyed him doubtfully. "But it's not your fight."

"It is now." He tucked a stray piece of hair behind my ear. "I want to help you, and not just tonight. I'll ride this thing to the end...wherever it goes."

"Regardless of whether it's good or bad?"

"Yes."

"I might as well tell you everything," I said quietly.

"There's more?"

I strolled across the room, stopping in front of the windows. I gazed into the darkness. Everything was a blur of colors that meant nothing. "I've been getting notes too."

I didn't hear his footsteps, but all of a sudden he stood behind me, his chest brushing against my back and his hands on my shoulders. His scent infiltrated my senses, soothing me. "What kind of notes? Is someone threatening you?"

"Yes. No. I don't know." I glanced over my shoulder, meeting his heavy-lidded gaze. His eyes glittered with rage. "The notes say to stay away from you and not to trust you."

He spun me around and cupped my face. He lowered his voice, indicating his words were only for me. "You can trust me. Those notes don't mean anything. Someone is trying to scare you. That's it. I'm not going to hurt you."

"You promise?"

"I promise."

I exhaled sharply. Archer said everything I needed to hear. Since my dad died, no one fought for me or stood up for what I wanted. What I needed. As a child, my dad and I were a team—us against the world. No matter what she did, my mom couldn't divide us. Then, his personal assistant found him dead in his bed one morning, and everything changed.

We moved across the country. I never saw my friends again. My dad's name never crossed my mom's lips. It was as if he never existed, and it was like losing him all over again.

The two years following my dad's death, I desperately sought my mom's approval and her love. I wanted her to fill my dad's shoes. It never happened. Then, she married my stepdad, and she never had a spare second for me. She focused all her thoughts and energy on maintaining his approval. There was no room for me in her new life. I was afterthought—an accessory to be pulled out of a drawer when the cameras rolled.

"And you and Knox have a plan?" I asked, glancing at Archer and then Knox.

Archer nodded. "We do. Are you ready to hear it?"

"I am."

CHAPTER TWENTY-ONE

Archer

"I don't know if I can do this," Langley said as she tied her shoes.

Langley had turned my world upside down with her confession last night. Some of the information I already knew, but the email gave Knox and me something we hadn't been able to find—an admission of sorts in Senator Wharton's own words. Now we had almost everything we needed to destroy his presidential hopes and send him to jail.

I sat down next to her on the bed. "You'll be fine. If you cancel, he'll be suspicious."

She flopped backward onto the bed, and her hair spilled over the side like a waterfall. My fingers itched to run through the silken strands, but I kept my hands firmly planted in my lap. If she didn't leave in the next five minutes, she'd be late, and I didn't want to make any mistakes now that I had my first real lead.

"You're right. I realize what's on the line here."

She rolled onto her side and then stood up. "I still don't understand why you won't come with me. I wouldn't be half as nervous if I didn't have to face them alone. I can't imagine how I'll keep my emotions in check." She visibly shivered. "Ugh. I don't want to talk to him. I can't imagine being in the same room with him. He makes me sick."

Guilt knotted my insides. I needed to come clean and tell her the truth. She put all her cards on the table, and I still held mine close to my chest, but every time I wanted to confess my connection to Senator Wharton, something stopped me...mainly my fear she'd switch sides if she knew the truth. It was selfish. I knew it. Knox told me as much after Langley went to bed last night, but I couldn't risk it when I was so close to the finish line.

"We both know why. We've gone over this at least five times already." And we had. Senator Wharton didn't want me in Langley's life. According to her, he didn't give much of a reason, but that could change if I showed up at his home.

"I know. He'd freak. It'd be a blatant show of disrespect." She laughed. "It almost makes me want to drag you along to see his face. For the most part, I've always done what they asked, so he'd be shocked."

I smiled and wrapped my arms around her waist. "I can drive you if it makes you feel any better. The minute you text me that you want to leave, I'll be waiting outside for you," I said quietly as I rubbed my hand along the back of her head. Her hair was still damp from her shower this morning, and the ends were starting to curl. Even without makeup and her hair disheveled she stole my breath.

She stepped out of my embrace and looked around my bedroom distractedly. "That isn't necessary. It's just a few hours and then I'll be out of there." She snagged her purse off my dresser and fished around inside for something.

"It's not a problem. I don't have any plans today except taking care of you. I can grab coffee or lunch somewhere nearby while I review some contracts for work."

"Are you sure you won't be bored? You've already done so much for me."

"I'll manage. Don't worry about me. Just concentrate on what you need to say to Senator Wharton today."

She nodded. "Thank God I took acting classes as a kid. I'll have to pull out all the stops."

"You took acting classes?" I asked, even though I knew everything about her short-lived acting career. All that information was part of the research Knox and I gathered before I met Langley. She appeared in a couple commercials, and she had a cameo role in an A-list film before her dad died, but nothing in the ten or so years since she and her mom relocated across the country.

Blushing, she glanced at the floor. "Yes. Before my dad died, I dreamed of following in his footsteps. I wanted do a film together." She shrugged. "It didn't work out, so I became a physical therapist."

"A natural transition," I joked.

"Not really, but I enjoy helping people and exercising. Physical therapy seemed like a good choice."

"Is it your passion?"

"I like it, and for now, that's good enough. Besides, my mom and stepdad always hated the idea of me pursuing an acting career."

"And they like the idea of you being a physical therapist?"

She scoffed. "Not even close. My mom thinks it's beneath me."

"What does she think you should do?"

Her eyebrows arched. "Honestly?"

"Honestly," I replied.

"I think she'd like me to marry some guy in politics, or with the potential to have a career in politics, and bounce from charity to charity offering my time and image for the greater good."

I gave her a wry glance. "So, in other words, she'd like you to follow in her footsteps."

She smirked. "Something like that. What about you?"

"What about me?"

"Is owning an investment firm your lifelong dream, or did you want to do something equally impractical as acting when you were a kid?"

I shoved my hands in my pockets. "I wanted to be successful. The method mattered less than the outcome." To an outsider who hadn't lived in a trailer park with threadbare clothing, my admission probably sounded mercenary, but it was the unvarnished truth. When my stomach ached with hunger, I wanted to end the misery any way I could, and that was enough of a dream to give me the courage to wake up every morning and live another day.

"That's it?"

I shifted on my feet. "That's it," I echoed, not wanting to put into words the rejection that fueled my childhood anger and propelled me to accomplish what I did over the last ten years. I'd built a company. I'd padded my bank account so I'd never have to experience the aching hunger that was the hallmark of my childhood, but most importantly, I'd made a name for myself—one that could stand toe to toe with Senator Wharton's. In a way, I should be thankful for Senator Wharton, because he provided the motive to channel my anger and misery into a ticket out of that shithole trailer park in Arizona. "Growing up in the hell Knox and I experienced on a daily basis didn't leave much room for dreams."

"With or without dreams, you both turned out pretty damn good in my opinion." She coiled her long hair into a bun, securing it at the back of her neck with a few well-placed pins. I preferred it tumbling down her back in long, golden waves. It made her look less like the icy princess photographed in pictures with her family.

"I'm glad you approve." I held out my hand to her. "Are you ready to go?"

"No." She laughed, but it sounded brittle and so unlike her.

"Hm," I said, pulling her close to me. "I think I need to help you relax a little."

She rolled her eyes. "Good luck with that. I feel like I'm about to crack in half from all the tension in my body."

Tentatively, I brushed my lips across hers, keeping my eyes open to gauge her reaction.

"Nope. That didn't help," she murmured under her breath as she backpedaled a step or two.

"Good, because I'm not done yet." I tugged her against me more firmly this time. In a few forceful strides, I had her backed against my dresser. I sealed my mouth over hers, deepening the pressure, demanding her surrender. When she finally relaxed, the addictive slide of her lips against mine sent sparks sliding down my spine, settling low in my gut. My tongue dipped into her parted mouth, and she moaned. Her sweet taste intoxicated me with every swirl.

At that moment, I realized I'd never get enough of Langley. My heart clenched painfully with bittersweet desire at the irrationality of the realization. Every second we spent together was a countdown to the end. We didn't have a future, which made me even more determined to take as much of the present as she'd give me.

I tunneled my hands through her hair, and the bun at the back of her head unraveled. Like an explosion, we were all over each other, caressing, stroking until we were both mindless. She rocked her hips against me, and I wanted to ignore everything we needed to do and crawl under her skin until she felt the ghost of my touch long after our relationship faded into a bitter memory.

When I finally pulled my mouth from hers, my lungs burned for oxygen, and judging from the clock on my wall, she'd be late, but her soft smile and unfocused gaze were worth the delay.

"Now I'm ready to go," she remarked, a laugh bubbling from her swollen lips.

I threaded my hand through hers. "Glad I could be of service."

CHAPTER TWENTY-TWO

Langley

"There's a problem," I said as I settled into the chair across from my stepdad at the kitchen table.

He looked up from his stack of papers and removed his wire-rimmed reading glasses, placing them on the table. "What are you talking about?"

I glanced over my shoulder and then leaned forward, supporting my elbows on the ash-colored table. "I found a listening device at my home." For the most part, I told the truth, except I didn't find it; Knox did.

He scrubbed his hand over his chin for a second, watching me with an unsettling intensity. "How do you know it's a listening device?"

I reached into my pocket and dropped my computer mouse on the center of the table. "It's inside there." My hands shook with fear and my lungs constricted. Since I met him at the age of twelve, my mind had turned him into this invincible, bigger than life man, with the clout to either annihilate me or exalt me. Time hadn't done a thing to mitigate that impression.

"Just this one. That's all you found?"

I swallowed hard, struggling to suppress the nausea swelling like a tidal wave in my gut. There were more, or at least according to Knox, but he didn't think we should remove every one of them from my house yet. "Yes, but I don't know. There could be more. I'm not an expert."

"How did you find this one?"

My stomach dropped to my knees. I didn't have an answer. Internally, I cursed Archer and Knox for not prepping me on this point. My legs tingled with the urge to run out of the house, but I forced myself to remain seated and finish the conversation. I exhaled as I ran my finger along the sharp edge of the table. "A friend found it. He used to work for the military or something. I'm not really sure. He said I should get someone to look at it, but I thought I should take it to you first," I said, keeping my story as close to the truth as possible. That way, I'd be less likely to stumble over details.

My stepdad picked up the mouse and twirled it in his fingers before dropping it into his briefcase, resting against the leg of his chair. "I'll have some of my people look at it to make sure. It might be nothing."

I nodded as I bounced my leg up and down under the table. "You're probably right. My friend wasn't totally sure anyway. I just wanted to bring it up with you." I leaned forward and lowered my voice. "Do you think someone is trying to get information about you?" I asked, my eyes wide and innocent, drawing on every last genetic acting ability I could muster.

"It's possible," he answered, tapping his fingers on the stack of papers in front of him.

"You really think so?"

"You can never be too safe."

"I don't know anything, so I guess it doesn't matter either way. It's just…" my voice trailed off, and I swallowed. "Creepy. You know? I don't feel safe in my home anymore."

"Have you been staying with a friend?"

"A couple nights, but I think I'll call Winnie and see if I can sleep on her couch."

"Your old room is always open to you. You can stay here until we get to the bottom of this."

I shook my head. "I couldn't inconvenience you and mom like that. I know you're busy right now. I'll just be in the way."

"No. It's actually a good idea. I'm going to announce my presidential campaign on Wednesday of next week from our living room. I'd love for you to be there."

"Oh, so soon?" I asked, wringing my numb, cold hands in my lap, striving to calm my frazzled nerves. I knew he planned to announce his candidacy any week, but Wednesday was only four days away. Four days—that's all the time we had to find a way to stop my stepdad. Archer didn't think the timing mattered as long as it happened before Senator Wharton was elected, but I didn't want this to drag on for weeks, much less months.

"Yes. My advisors already scheduled the interview. We had a few stumbling blocks to overcome, but everything came together seamlessly." My stepdad stood up and shoved his hand in his perfectly starched khaki trousers. "You know, the more I think about it, the more I like the idea of having you move back in for a while."

"I don't think—"

"It'd be perfect. Brandon is staying here for the next couple of days to strategize and take care of any loose ends. You guys can reconnect. I never understood why you two broke up. Your mom and I like him. He's a good man."

"No," I snapped before I could moderate my voice. "I can't do it."

He cocked his head to the side. "You can't? What does that mean?"

"Brandon and I aren't on the best of terms. It'd be awkward, and I don't want to be a distraction for him. I know you rely on him. It wouldn't be fair." What the hell! Why was Brandon getting closer to my stepdad rather than running as far and as fast as he could from him? Brandon suspected my stepdad was monitoring him and his calls. It didn't make sense.

"Really?" Smiling faintly, he walked toward the gleaming white and gray veined marble countertop across the kitchen. He poured a cup of coffee. "That's interesting. I thought you two were in the process of reconciling."

"No, that's not going to happen."

He held up a white empty mug with his elegant fingers that had never done a day of manual labor. "Would you like some coffee?"

"No." I shook my head, refusing his offer even

though it would probably help my suddenly shivering body. I didn't want to prolong this visit any longer than necessary. In fact, there was no way I was staying to play tennis with my mom today. "I'm good. I already had two cups this morning."

"Hm, that's strange," he mumbled as he circled behind my chair.

I swiveled in my chair not wanting my back to him. "What's strange?"

"I thought you and Brandon met last weekend to work things out."

"Last weekend?" My heart thundered in my chest, drowning out the sound of my voice.

His hands dropped on my shoulder, and my muscles tensed. I bit my lower lip as disgust coiled around my stomach like a snake. It took every ounce of willpower I could rally in the recesses of my soul not to jerk away from his vile touch. Instead of making a scene, I counted like I always did when I thought I was going to snap.

One.

Two.

Three.

Four.

Five.

"Yes. I thought you two met last weekend near the Lincoln Memorial." He removed his hands and settled into the chair next to me on the count of six. I sucked in a breath. "Am I wrong?"

I stared at him, at the man I once considered my family, not uttering a single word for a tense hair-raising second. Hate didn't begin to describe the visceral reaction I had to him. It was too simple of a

174

word. "Yes, we did, but not because we had any intention of getting back together." I barely managed to keep the panic out of my voice. Just as Brandon had warned me, my stepdad had people watching every step I took and every word I muttered.

"Then why did you meet?" he said with a sigh.

"He found something of mine that I left at his house," I answered. I kept my voice deceptively calm in order to conceal the horrors spinning through my mind one after another, each one crazier and more demented than the last.

"What?" One eyebrow lifted in sync with his one-word question.

"Excuse me?"

His mouth contorted into a chilly, ironic smile that told me more than his words. "What did you leave at his house?" he asked again.

I glanced to the side. This conversation had taken a strange twist, and there was only one explanation for it—he knew that I knew about those ten women. Well, fuck him. He wanted to make me squirm under his interrogation. It may have worked last week, but it wouldn't work now. I forced a bright smile on my face and offered an equally uncomfortable response. "Personal items." I shrugged. "You know...feminine hygiene products, makeup, underwear, birth control pills. After six months, I still hadn't stopped by to pick up the things I left at his house. I told him to throw them away, but he wouldn't do it. Why are you asking?" I laughed, pretending as though I didn't suspect a thing, that his questions weren't bizarre given our virtually non-existent relationship.

He looked at me oddly for a second. Then a rueful smile spread across his face. "No reason."

I glanced at my watch. "Crap," I said, shaking my head. "I can't stay to play tennis with mom. I promised I'd meet Winnie for lunch in thirty minutes. Can you tell her I'm sorry?"

"Sure."

Pushing my chair away from the table, the hind legs scratched across the wood floor and the dishes on the table jangled. "I'll probably see you next Saturday, but I'm not sure."

"I'd still like you to be here on Wednesday."

I stood up. "Oh, right. I forgot about your announcement. What time?"

"Five in the afternoon."

I nodded. "That might be difficult. I can't promise anything, but I'll see if I can reschedule my last patient."

"It was nice seeing you."

"Yes," I answered, my voice flat.

I held up my open palm and waved awkwardly, and then fled the room. The rubber soles of my shoes squeaked on the smooth flooring as I rushed through the house to the front door as fast as possible without breaking into a full run, but that changed the minute I slammed the door to their home.

My feet slapped against the concrete as I ran without purpose or plan, driven solely by the need to escape my stepdad as quickly as possible. He managed to obliterate any sliver of doubt I harbored of his innocence. He didn't say anything too damning, but my instincts screamed he was guilty of everything Brandon suspected and more.

I brushed by people lingering on the street, ignoring their questioning stares. I'm sure I looked crazed with hot tears spilling down my cheeks. I didn't have the luxury of worrying what people thought. I was living in a nightmare.

I didn't bother to text Archer to pick me up until I'd put four solid blocks between my stepdad and me. As I stood on the corner, shivering both from the cold and the chat with my stepfather, the wind howled, blowing my hair around my face and drying my salty tears. I didn't care. I felt oddly empty. I waited for the anger, the sadness, the disappointment...anything. But nothing came. My emotions had gone on a hiatus to a quiet, dark place in a secret alcove of my soul, leaving me utterly and blessedly numb.

CHAPTER TWENTY-THREE

Archer

"He knows," Langley said the minute she slipped into the backseat of the car next to me.

"What does he know?" Langley texted me to pick her up around the corner from Senator Wharton's house ten minutes ago. I hadn't expected her to finish for another hour, so I had stopped by Knox's house to go over the final details of our plan.

Her head rolled forward, and she covered her face with her hands. "Everything. I'm sure of it."

My heart lurched in my chest and my muscles stiffened. "Everything?" Her definition of everything was vastly different from his, but I wouldn't have been surprised if he told her a lot of things I didn't want her to know about me just yet.

She dropped her hands, her face void of emotion. "Yes."

I nodded, waiting for her to scramble across the seat and put as much space between us as possible, but she didn't. Instead, she turned her head, resting it against my shoulder. I could feel the wetness of her tears against my shirt.

I trailed my fingers through the tangled waves of her hair. "Can you be more specific?"

"He knows I met Brandon last week."

"That doesn't mean anything," I pointed out, even though it confirmed that Senator Wharton was watching Langley's movements.

"It means he's watching me." Her voice splintered on the last word. "I think he asked me about it because he wants me to know he's watching me."

"Perhaps, but you already knew, so it shouldn't have been a surprise."

She lifted her head and stared at me. "You're right, but part of me wanted to believe he could still be innocent, or that this was a misunderstanding."

"You read the email. You heard Brandon's warning."

"I did."

"But you still hoped it would all disappear, or he'd be able to explain it away." I waited for a denial, but it never came.

"I did. My mom hasn't been much of a parent, and my stepdad didn't care about me except when I played the doting stepdaughter on the campaign trail, but I still had a family. Now I don't. I can't participate in their life. I can't pretend I have people in the world who care about me." She shook her head. "I have Winnie. She'll always be my friend, but it doesn't seem like enough."

"You have me." It was the naked truth. Unfortunately, she wouldn't want me when she discovered the depth of my depravity. Everything between us started as a carefully orchestrated lie, but somehow all the lies twisted and turned until they morphed into the truth. I cared about Langley more than I should, more than was wise given the inevitable outcome of our relationship. We were a real live Shakespearean tragedy in the making.

Her cat-like eyes met mine, her cheeks shimmering with the salt of her dried tears and her nose red from standing in the cold. Even now, she looked beautiful. "Do I?"

"I promised I'd help you and I will," I murmured, resting my head against hers.

She leaned her head against my shoulder again, and my gut twisted with guilt. Every ounce of my soul begged me to tell her the truth, but the words never came. I didn't know where to start.

"For some reason I believe you. Maybe that makes me stupid, but I think you're my best option. My only option."

It took me a long time to respond. "I'm not going to let you down," I whispered as I brushed a kiss on top of her head. I wanted to believe my declaration. I wanted to be her savior even though I knew she should get the hell away from Senator Wharton and me. If I weren't so selfish, I would've demanded she leave D.C. I should've packed her bags for her and booked her a one way ticket to somewhere far, far away from me, but I didn't. Shaking my head, I buried my sense of right and wrong again.

"What's the plan now, Archer? Do I go back to my place and pretend nothing has happened? That I'm not being monitored? That he's not watching every single thing I do?" She sounded lost and void of emotion, as though she'd reached the end of her endurance. She no longer cared how I answered her questions.

"We're going to take a vacation."

"What?" She lifted her head from my shoulder. "Why would we do that?"

"Because you need time to recoup," I answered simply.

"But he plans to announce his candidacy on Wednesday. That's only four days away."

I shrugged. "That's plenty of time."

"Are you crazy? We need to figure something out, and we'll need every minute of those four days to do it."

"A couple days won't matter. We almost have everything we need." Knox already had everything in place. The email provided all the details he needed to puzzle the whole thing together. By the end of the weekend, his team will have finished interviewing every living woman on the list. He'd have copies of the nondisclosure agreements and as much evidence as possible linking Senator Wharton to the three dead women. By Saturday evening, the Senator would be in receipt of a letter outlining his options. If he refused to comply, the information would be leaked to the press at six in the morning on Tuesday. His Wednesday announcement will never happen.

"How?"

"I talked to Knox. He doesn't need our help. This is his area of expertise, and he'll be much more efficient if we get out of his way."

She tapped her finger against her lips. "A vacation is your idea of getting out of his way?"

"Yes. It makes sense. You'll get some relaxation before the storm hits, and if we're lucky, you'll escape Senator Wharton's surveillance for a couple of days, which gives him less opportunity to become suspicious of you."

"And if I don't want to get out of Knox's way and go on a vacation?" she said stubbornly, but I didn't miss the smile playing at the corner of her lips.

"I'll force you."

Her eyebrows lifted, and she laughed, which was so much better than the emotional black hole she'd been in since she got into the car. "Really? I'd like to see that. Will you tie my hands and feet and throw me into the car?"

I shrugged and smoothed her hair away from her face. "If I have to, but I have a feeling it won't come to that when you find out where I plan to take you."

"Where are you taking me?"

"To a resort and spa near the Bull Run Mountains in Virginia."

"I see," she said, a full-blown smile on her face now. "What will we do there?"

"Nothing. Everything. Whatever you want."

"Unlimited spa treatments?"

"If that's what you want to do."

Her brows furrowed. "And what will you do?"

"Enjoy watching you have a good time," I said, my voice soft and aching with more vulnerability than I liked.

"That's it?"

"Isn't that enough?" I asked, unable to stop myself. My chest ached with the realization that watching her was more than enough for me.

She shook her head. "You confuse me." She waved her hand back and forth between us. "This thing between us, whatever it is, confuses me, but in a good way."

"How so?" I asked, not even sure if I wanted the answer.

"Because you always know how to make me feel better. It's almost as if we've known each other for years rather than a month or so. When I'm with you, none of this mess with my stepdad seems so bad anymore." Her smile and voice were almost dreamy with reverence.

I bent to kiss her—a sweet, gentle kiss that told her without words how much she meant to me.

How much I ached for her.

How I'd never craved any woman as much as I craved her.

How I'd never stop wanting her even when she stopped wanting me.

All my wealth and lengthy list of accomplishments didn't mean anything. She'd given me something I'd never had before...something I thought I'd never have. She gave me a new home, a new outlook on life, a new everything. I'd spent the first part of my life wanting revenge, but at that moment, I knew I'd spend the rest of my life wanting to make her happy.

CHAPTER
TWENTY-FOUR

Langley

"Langley." A hand closed around my upper arm. I shifted in my seat.

I heard a deep chuckle next my ear, but I ignored it and brushed the hand away. "Leave me alone," I mumbled, not opening my heavy eyes.

"Langley, we're here. Wake up."

I opened my eyes, blinked a few times, and then turned my head to the side. "Where?"

"The hotel."

I flipped the visor down, studying my face. "What time is it?"

"Four in the afternoon."

"Oh my God, I slept the entire way."

"I noticed. If I'd known you didn't plan to keep me company, I would've had the driver take us. At least I could've taken care of some work," he teased, his fully dimpled smile on display.

185

"Sorry," I groaned as I stretched my arms above my head and glanced out the window. My mouth dropped open when I saw the view in front of me. A two-story brick hotel with two wings and an inviting white portico sat directly in front of me, surrounded by acres and acres of impeccably manicured lawn and wooded rolling hills. "It's beautiful," I murmured.

"You've never been here before?"

"No. My mom goes here with her girlfriends every year, but I've never gone with her. Winnie and I booked a weekend getaway here a couple months ago, but her work cut back her hours and we canceled the trip."

"Well, then I'm glad I picked this place."

While Archer checked into the hotel, I roamed the main floor taking in all the traditional details. The lobby impressed me as much as the exterior of the hotel. Light blue walls complimented the ivory and tan furnishings. Paintings of horses lined the walls, reflecting the equestrian heritage of that region of Virginia. A California girl at heart, I'd much rather ride the waves than a horse, but I appreciated the beauty of the setting and the lifestyle.

"Are you ready to go to our room, or would you like to walk around awhile?" Archer asked, wrapping an arm around my waist.

"I'd much rather go to the room."

"Then, we're on the same page," he said with a smirk as he guided me toward the elevator.

My heart clenched at his subtle insinuation. Two uninterrupted days with Archer started now, and I had every intention of concentrating on him instead of dwelling on the coming storm with my stepdad. The impending scandal and media frenzy could wait.

Two minutes later, Archer and I stepped into our room. The colors and décor from the lobby seamlessly transitioned into the rooms, and I already felt much lighter and carefree than I had in weeks.

"Thank you," I said, circling my arms around his neck.

"For what?" He smiled down at me, his darker than sin eyes hooded but filled with amusement.

"For taking me here. For getting me out of D.C. for a couple days. For helping me with this whole mess. I'm so lucky you found me hiding in the hallway at that stupid fundraiser."

He cupped my face almost reverently. "I'm the lucky one. I haven't had a vacation in months. Now, I'm at a five star hotel with a gorgeous and intelligent woman."

I shook my head back and forth once, but not hard enough to break his light hold on my face. "For the first time in my life, I truly feel blessed. Someone is watching over me."

He cocked his head to the side, his lips curling into a lopsided grin. "Someone?"

"Yes, and that someone is you—"

He pressed two fingers over my mouth, interrupting my confession. "Shh, Langley. I don't want to talk now."

"You don't?" I muttered against the tips of his fingers.

"No," he answered simply, dropping his hands from my face.

"Then, what do you want to do?"

"This," he murmured, cementing his declaration with a kiss.

My palms flattened against the contours of his muscular chest as his lips moved back and forth across mine, engulfing me in a blistering heat with every hypnotic glide of his mouth. His lips, teeth, and tongue collided with mine, fusing us together, not leaving a single area untouched. Dizzy, my hands dropped to my sides and I swayed into him. His heart thumped strong and steady against my chest, beating in time with mine.

Claimed.

Possessed.

Loved.

That's how I felt at that instant. Those primal thoughts should have sent me running as fast and as far as I could from Archer, but everything about Archer and this moment felt absolutely right.

Even though I hadn't been able to count on anyone in my past, I believed Archer could be the person to change the pattern.

My dad chose drugs.

My mom chose my stepdad.

Brandon chose his job.

But Archer…he chose me.

In that glimmer of time, with Archer claiming my soul and my body, thoughts of my stepdad, Brandon, and the coming week faded into nothingness, which pleased me more than I could ever convey. I didn't want to think about the bad in my life. I wanted to embrace the good, and that meant living in the present with Archer.

The kiss went on and on until the back of my thighs smacked the side of the mattress, and I tumbled backward, finally separating our lips. I sucked a mouthful of air into my oxygen-starved lungs, watching and waiting for his next move.

Color stained his sharp-angled cheekbones, his chest heaved with every breath, and his brown eyes glimmered with arousal. His dark beauty took my breath away.

"Langley," he hummed through his teeth. The sound of my name spoken from his pleasure-stung lips vibrated over my nerve endings, setting them on fire with a bone-aching lust only he brought out in me.

"Archer," I whispered. My body thrummed with awareness as his gaze raked over my prone body. His dilated pupils lingered on my face as he released the button and zipper of my pants with a skillful flick of his wrist. The smooth pads of his fingers whispered over the small expanse of exposed skin, and a shudder whistled through my body.

He gripped my hips and slid my pants down my legs. A dark tide swallowed me as his lips traced the inside of one thigh, then the other. I wanted him so badly; I couldn't speak. I couldn't move.

"Take off your shirt," he demanded, visually devouring me.

Nodding, I lifted it over my head and tossed it on the bed beside me. Now, I sat on the bed in only my bra and matching panties.

"I like these," he said, one finger toying with the lace edge of my panties. The rawness of his voice sent a tremor of desire down my spine. "But they have to go." He yanked the wisp of lace down my legs.

He bent my legs one at a time, positioning them on the bed too far apart to ignore his intent. A blush crept up my face. As much as I wanted to hide from his penetrating gaze, I couldn't look away. His eyes flared with heat as his mouth closed over my sex. Arousal roared through my body like I had gasoline for blood and Archer was the spark.

Within seconds, not minutes, I was lost, spiraling faster and faster toward my release. I tried to hold back, to stop it, but it wasn't possible. My eyes slammed shut, and I embraced the sensations whipping through my body with every stroke of his skilled tongue and mouth. Air escaped my lungs in a greedy moan, and my entire body stiffened. He slid two fingers inside of me, and I exploded.

"Archer," I screamed as my entire body shuddered. It went on and on, so long that when I finally opened my eyes, Archer stood in front of me completely naked, rolling on a condom. I consumed him with my eyes, committing every detail to memory.

His broad chest.

His narrow waist.

His muscular thighs.

His sexy dimple.

Leaning forward, he unclasped my bra and slid it down my shoulders. "Are you ready?"

I wrapped my arms around his neck and pulled

his mouth to mine. His tongue slid against mine, stroking me until I ached with need to be filled by him.

Like he could read my mind, he pressed into me. I gasped at the perfection of the moment...at the perfection of him inside of me.

"Perfect," I mumbled. The words tumbled from my mouth unwittingly.

"My thoughts exactly."

My stomach clenched as his velvety voice vibrated on my skin like a caress. The world around us disappeared. In that flash of time, it was the two of us moving together, and nothing else mattered.

His hips moved back and forth, each thrust deeper than the last, coaxing another orgasm from me with every flex of his hips. His mouth found mine again. I arched against him, lost in his relentless rhythm. Lost in the moment. Lost in the sensation of Archer moving inside of me. I forgot about all my worries. I didn't care about anything except the release shimmering just outside of my reach.

He adjusted my hips, just a small movement, but it made all the difference. An intense, mind-splitting sensation rippled through me. I cried out, digging my hands into his hips, pulling him closer to me, demanding everything he had to offer and more. Within seconds, he slammed inside of me one last time, curses falling from his lips and sweat beading on his brow as his body shuddered.

He lowered his head against the crook of my neck as our hearts drummed in harmony. I shivered, and Archer pulled the blanket over our entwined bodies. He kissed my neck and then my lips, and rolled over.

His lips curled into a smile. "A whole weekend together," he whispered, our eyes meeting in a moment of perfect intimacy.

"Just like this," I said, my voice already thick with exhaustion.

"No." He knitted his fingers through mine and laughed softly. "I promise to feed you once in a while too."

I laughed, letting my eyes drift closed. "How thoughtful."

"No, just greedy. I can't have you pass out on me." He wound his arm around my waist and pulled me back against his chest. "Go to sleep."

CHAPTER TWENTY-FIVE

Archer

"Is Knox your only family?"

I rolled my head to the side and ran my finger along her jaw. Langley had been firing questions at me since we woke up this morning. I didn't mind. For the first time in my life, I wanted to share my past with someone. No, not someone. Langley.

Over the last twenty-four hours, she erased all my memories of the faceless women who came before her. There was only Langley, her golden hair, her million-dollar smile, and her sexy green eyes.

"We have another brother. He's eight years younger than me," I answered. I never discussed Gunnar with anyone. Our relationship was complicated.

"Are you close?"

"Not really. We trade phone calls every couple

months, but I haven't seen him for over a year, maybe more."

Her green eyes brimmed with curiosity. "Why?"

"He went to live with his dad's family when he was six years old."

Her brows furrowed. "How'd that happen?"

"Our mom wasn't much of a mom, and his dad wasn't much of a dad, but his dad came from money. My mom didn't come home for days at a time, and she'd leave Gunnar alone with Knox and me. When Gunnar's grandparents realized what was happening, they fought my mom for custody, and they won easily."

"I'm sure it was hard to be separated from your brother."

"It was the best thing for Gunnar. He lived with a stable family. I can't say the same thing about Knox and me."

"Where's you mom now?"

"She died."

Langley threaded her fingers through mine and squeezed my hand. "How?"

"The police report said she killed herself," I answered, even though I didn't believe it, especially now.

"I know it's silly to say, but I'm sorry. You probably know my dad died of an overdose." She closed her eyes. "I've never really come to terms with it. There are days when I wake up angry with him for choosing the drugs over me. Then, other days I'm just sad he's not here. At every milestone, I feel the pain of his death again." She opened her eyes and shook her head. "It's a hole in my heart that will never be filled no matter how many days pass."

Reaching out, I brushed her hair from her face, but it was more of an excuse to touch her, not that I needed one. She was mine...for now. "I understand how you feel about your dad choosing drugs over you. Until a few months before she died, my mom was a somewhat functioning alcoholic. Growing up, if she had to choose between putting food on the table or buying a bottle of vodka, the vodka always won."

"What about your dad? Are you close?"

"No," I spat before I could restrain my instinctive reaction to him. I didn't want to talk about him now with Langley next to me in bed. I wanted to leave all our baggage back in D.C. This weekend was about us, for us. Period.

"Why not?"

"He wasn't interested in having a relationship with me. The feelings are mutual."

"Not even now that you're so successful?"

"I don't want to talk about him."

She nodded. "I get it. I don't like to talk about my dad either." Sitting up, she kissed me lightly on the lips. "Since we didn't do anything yesterday, what should we do today?"

"Hm." I grabbed her by the waist and yanked her on top of me. Her shirt gaped, offering me a clear view of her breasts. "I'm confused. I distinctly remember doing something yesterday."

A blush stained her cheeks, and she playfully smacked my chest. "You know what I mean."

"No, I really don't." I slid my hands under the

hem of her silky camisole.

"Not now." She laughed. "We'll never leave this room."

"And what's wrong with that?"

"We need to be productive and do something else, or at least for a little while."

The pads of my fingers skated along the undersides of her breasts. "Was there something wrong with what we did yesterday? If so, we can try again."

She grabbed my forearms, restraining my movements. "It was perfect and you know it."

"Good. In that case, I thought we'd go horseback riding today."

"No," she groaned.

"Bad choice?"

"It's not my thing. My mom put me in lessons when we left California, but I wasn't very good."

"No?" I questioned.

"No." She lowered her voice. "I'm afraid of horses," she confessed.

"Why?"

She lifted and then dropped one shoulder. "They're big. They buck. They kick. They bite. What's not to be afraid of?"

"Then, we'll share a horse."

"I don't know if that's a good idea."

"Trust me. I'm good with horses."

One eyebrow lifted. "Really?"

"Yep. My brother taught me everything I know."

"Knox?"

"No. Gunnar. He breeds racehorses."

She eyed me skeptically, and I tugged her closer

to me. "But you haven't seen him in two years."

"Knox and I spent two weeks every summer at his grandparents' horse farm before we went to college. Knox, Gunnar, and I rode horses until every muscle ached, but we didn't care. Those two weeks were the best part of my childhood. That and Christmas were the only days we spent with Gunnar every year, so we made the best of it."

"That's not a lot of time."

"No. You're right, but my mom didn't request anything else. That's all she wanted."

"You don't think she cared."

"She knew her limitations. My mom couldn't even take care of herself most days, much less two or three kids. Knox and I were lucky if we had one meal a day. She didn't care if we went to school. Hell, half the time she didn't even come home at night."

I didn't want to get into the gritty details with Langley. From the little my mom shared of her childhood, I understood why she ended up on the streets at the age of sixteen. Within two months, an escort service recruited her, and by seventeen, she found herself broke and pregnant with me. After that, things went from bad to worse.

According to my mom, the man who fathered me paid her a lump sum of one hundred thousand dollars to keep quiet and take care of my needs. She blew through the money in a year and a half. She was back to selling her body for money and pregnant with Knox not long after that.

My mom claimed she didn't know how to find Knox's biological father. According to her, it was just one night, and no names were exchanged. Knox didn't believe her, and I didn't know if I did either.

"That's sad."

"Don't feel sorry for us. It wasn't a big deal. "

She shook her head. "I don't. I'm angry you had to endure a life like that. No child should go without food."

Feeling exposed in a way I hadn't since I left our shitty trailer to go to college over ten years ago, I lifted her off my lap and sat her on the bed next to me. I had to remember this thing with Langley was temporary.

"We all turned out fine, so I guess she made the right decision. No harm done." I stood up and walked toward the bathroom. "We need to be at the stables in an hour," I said, desperate to change the direction of our conversation. I already said too much. Revealed too much.

Taking my hint, she leaped up. "I'll skip the shower until after we're done horseback riding. I'd rather eat breakfast."

"Sounds good to me."

CHAPTER TWENTY-SIX

Langley

After an hour of paperwork, we were settled atop a butter-colored horse with a black mane and tail. I sat in front of Archer, my hands on the horn of the saddle, and he held the reins directing the horse. Somehow Archer managed to convince the supervisor to let us ride alone. As we wove in and out of the still barren trees, Archer directed the horse with subtle flexes of his thighs and movements of the reins.

Not many people were riding horses or hiking the trails on foot. Most likely, the heavy fog kept them back at the hotel instead of roaming the trails. Not that I had any intention of complaining. The further the horse carried us into the foothills of the Blue Ridge Mountains, the more I felt like it was just the two of us riding through an enchanted forest.

"Did Gunnar teach you how to ride?" I asked as we ducked under a low-hanging branch.

Archer chuckled. "I don't know if I'd consider what he did teaching."

I glanced over my shoulder, glimpsing a half-smile on his face. "Then, what would you call it?"

"The first year Knox and I visited him at his grandparents' house, he showed us the stables. He climbed on his horse and rode it in circles around the corral. He was only seven or eight years old. Knox and I had never even seen a horse in person, but when he asked us if we knew how to ride, we couldn't say no."

"Why not?"

"You don't know anything about brothers, do you?" he murmured, his lips right next to my ear. His warm breath made me acutely aware of the connection between our bodies. His muscular legs cradled my hips, brushing against me as he guided the horse through the woods.

"Not really. I was an only child."

"We couldn't admit that our younger brother was able to do something better than us."

"Please tell me you didn't climb on a horse without any instruction," I asked incredulously.

"We did. Well, technically, Knox went first."

"And what happened?" I prompted.

"Knox climbed on top of the horse and dug his heels into the horse's sides so hard, it bucked and he fell off."

"Oh my God. Was he hurt?"

"Not too bad."

"What does that mean?"

"He cracked his collarbone, and he had to wear a sling for a couple weeks, but he was fine."

"What about you? Did you fare any better?"

"I didn't fall off the horse," Archer answered evasively.

"Thank God."

He slipped his hand around my waist and pulled me closer to him. "The horse didn't move when I got on it."

"Why not?"

"I wasn't going to kick my heels into the horse's side and risk falling off."

"So you sat there."

"Pretty much. I sat in the saddle for a few minutes and then climbed right back down. I think I told him it was boring."

"Liar."

"Pretty much. Luckily, his grandfather gave us lessons the next day when Gunnar was out with his grandmother. Neither Knox nor I have Gunnar's innate skill with horses, but we can hold our own."

"I can tell."

"Do you want to stop here and eat lunch?"

"Sure."

Archer had the restaurant prepare two sandwiches for us. By the time we finished getting dressed this morning, we only had time to drink a cup of coffee and eat a banana.

He reined our horse to an immediate stop and it pranced in a tight circle. Bending over me, he stroked the horse's neck, whispering words of encouragement. When our mount stilled, he swung his right leg over its rear and jumped to the ground.

201

"Do you need some help?" he asked.

"Definitely." I laughed. With my arms twined around his neck, he grabbed my hips and pulled me toward him. My body pressed into his chest as I slid from the saddle. Lowering his head, he brushed his lips against mine. My breath caught in my throat, and my eyes drifted closed. I leaned into the hard planes of his body, and my lips parted, molding against his mouth. His heart drummed steady and strong against mine. I could get used to this. Used to having Archer in my life. Used to his touch. Used to the feel of his body next to mine.

A loud popping noise cracked above my head, and I jumped, pressing my back into the side of the horse. The sound thundered through the air again, and bark splintered into hundreds of tiny pieces on the tree behind me, showering my head. The horse reared onto his hind legs. Realizing we were in danger, Archer slapped the horse's flank, and it sprinted down the trail, its reins dangling in the dirt. He snagged my wrist and yanked me to the ground on all fours.

"What's going on?" I whispered.

"Those were gunshots."

My heart sputtered. "Gunshots? Why would someone shoot at us?"

"I don't know. It could be a hunter, but it isn't hunting season."

"Do you really believe that?" Another shot splintered the tree above our head.

"It doesn't matter what I believe right now. We need to move."

I bit down hard on my lip and my heart galloped

a million miles per hour in my chest. Frozen with fear, I couldn't move from the damp earth. I wanted to throw up. I forced air into my lungs, straining to pull myself together, but it felt like a thousand needles pressed into my chest. "I'm too scared to move," I rasped.

"You can be scared when we make it back to the hotel in one piece. Right now, we need to run."

I nodded, because I didn't have a choice if I wanted to live, and I did. "You lead. I'll follow."

Just then, a volley of shots pierced through the air one after another, each one closer than the last.

"Fuck," Archer hissed. "On the count of three, we're going to run into the trees behind us. It will provide us more cover than running down the trail."

"Okay," I said, my voice thick with fear.

"One." He laced his fingers through mine. "Two." He yanked me to my feet in one fluid movement. "Three." We both ran.

Twigs snapped under my shoes. Branches whipped my face. Blood roared in my ears. My shoulder burned from Archer pulling me by the arm, but I refused to let go of his hand. I ran until my lungs burned, barely dodging the trees. I was in good shape, but I never had to run to save my life. I didn't dare turn around, and neither did Archer. Sporadic gunshots split through the air. I counted each one, silently in my head, trying to calm my racing thoughts.

One.

Two.

Three.

Four.

Five.

Then, the gunshots disappeared entirely.

Ten minutes later, Archer stopped running, and I slammed into his back. We tumbled to the ground, rolling down the hill. My frazzled mind watched, almost detached from reality as a confusing mix of dirt, leaves, and tree limbs swirled in front of my eyes.

When our bodies stopped rolling, I sat up. I saw a stretch of grass and the hotel not too far in the distance.

"We made it," I whispered, my raspy voice raw from a combination of fear and exhaustion. Somehow Archer led us back to the hotel.

Archer pulled me against him, our panting breaths echoing in the stillness of the late afternoon. "I'm sorry. We should've stayed in the hotel today. Gone to the spa. Anything but horseback riding."

"It's not your fault. How could you know we'd end up in someone's crosshairs?"

Archer stepped back and rubbed his temples wearily. "I should've anticipated something like this."

"You don't think it was coincidence?" I said, my stomach churning uncomfortably.

"No," he said, his face pinched with anger. "Knox delivered a warning to Senator Wharton last night."

"Oh," I mumbled, dropping my gaze to the ground. "Do you think he had something to do with this?"

With athletic grace, he unfolded his body and stood up. He brushed the dirt from his pants. "It's possible. Very possible," he said, his eyes darkening. "We already know he doesn't have a problem killing people who get in his way."

His voice was distant, and I wondered if this whole thing with my stepdad was too much for him. Did he want to walk away? Did he regret promising to help me? I rested my head on my knees, unable to look at him. All these thoughts of his inevitable abandonment made me anxious.

"You don't have to go through with this. I won't be mad if you want out." I shook my head as I inhaled sharply. "This is a fucking disaster." My throat seized around the words, and my voice sounded rusty and hesitant. I didn't know what I'd do if he abandoned me, but I couldn't force him to stay by my side and endanger his life.

Archer sighed and held out his hand. "I don't want out."

"Are you sure?"

"Yes. You couldn't get rid of me if you wanted to."

I grabbed his outstretched hand, and he hauled me to my feet. I brushed the dirt off my jeans, wincing from the pain in my shoulder. "Fine, but you have to promise me one thing."

"What's that?" he asked with one eyebrow lifted.

"You won't force me to go horseback riding ever again," I deadpanned.

His lips twitched. "You've got it." He cocked his head to the side. "Although I reserve the right to try to change your mind in the future."

"It's a deal."

He brushed his knuckles along the side of my

face. "Are you ready to walk back to the hotel, or do you want to rest?"

I shivered at the thought of sitting out in the open, waiting for whomever to find us again. "No. Let's get the hell out of here. I've had enough outdoor activities for the day."

A soft smile tugged at the corner of his lips, and he pressed a barely-there kiss to my forehead. "Agreed."

As we walked toward the hotel, he looped his arm around my waist, drawing me flush against his body. I couldn't shake the feeling he was trying to safeguard me from something. I didn't mind. I rested my head on his shoulder and inhaled his spicy-citrus scent, committing it to memory. Despite everything that happened today, I felt cherished, wanted, and safe. It'd been a long time since I'd felt that way. I wanted to drink in every last moment. So many thoughts gathered on the tip of my tongue. I needed to tell him how much he meant to me. How much I cared about him.

CHAPTER TWENTY-SEVEN

Archer

"Knox, it's me." I sat down on the edge of the bed.

"I know. I have caller ID. How's the vacation going?" Knox asked.

My eyes flickered to the bathroom door. Langley had turned on the shower five minutes ago, so I didn't have much time to chat. "Not so good. Somebody fired shots at us while we were horseback riding."

"You're kidding," Knox said.

"I wish I were. I didn't even have a fucking gun to shoot back. I left it in the car."

"That was dumb. I told you to keep it within reach at all times. Maybe you'll listen to me in the future," Knox replied.

"I'll keep that in mind."

"Right. I won't hold my breath." Knox chuckled.

"So I take it both of you are okay."

"I was wondering when you were going to ask."

"Whatever. I told you this whole impromptu vacation was a dumb idea. You should be back here working on this with me."

"Have you made any progress?" I said, redirecting the conversation.

"Don't worry. I have all the evidence we need. His presidential campaign is dead in the water as of yesterday."

I leaned forward, resting my elbows on my knees. "What do you have?"

"Sworn testimony, pictures, and a fifteen-minute video. It's enough to end his career, maybe more."

"That was quick."

"My team interviewed all of the women. One of them agreed to sign an affidavit describing her interactions with Senator Wharton. Then, I hacked into Senator Wharton's personal computer. He actually had video stream and pictures of himself in compromising positions with those women."

"Wait." I shook my head. "Will he know his computer was hacked?"

"No. I used a module designed to reprogram or reflash the computer hard drive's firmware with malicious code."

"The firmware? How does that work?"

"It's brilliant. He'll never realize anyone has been on his computer. Once I replaced the firmware with a Trojanized version, the flasher module produced an application-programming interface with the ability to communicate with other malicious modules on the system—"

"Okay. Stop. That's more information than I ever wanted to know." Once Knox started talking about computers, he didn't stop.

Knox snorted. "That's how I feel when you talk about interest rate hikes and currency exchange rates."

"I'll remember that when you ask for more money." I always gave him a hard time about money, but he was worth every dollar.

"You pay me to prevent security breaches at Black Investments. You haven't had a single one."

"I know. I know." I leaned back and raked my hands through my hair. "Do you think Senator Wharton hired someone to kill us?" I asked, even though I didn't have any doubts.

"I can check it out, make some phone calls, but I wouldn't be surprised." Knox didn't say anything for a few minutes, and I didn't push him. Knox only revealed what he wanted. "It's not too late to walk away from this. There are other women out there, ones who aren't related to that asshole."

I squeezed my eyes shut, trying to imagine a life without Langley, but all I could see was her.

Her golden hair sprawled out on my pillow.

Her smile melting the ice prison around my heart.

Her green eyes glowing with trust.

I shook my head even though he couldn't see me. "No, I can't do that."

"You're being stupid. Incredibly stupid."

"Since when do you care who I date?" I snapped.

"Since the woman you're dating comes with a possible expiration date on your life."

"This isn't Langley's fault. I forced my way into her life, not the other way around."

"Then, force your way out of her life before it's too fucking late. This isn't a game. Senator Wharton won't hesitate to kill you or her. The clock is ticking on his political career, and he knows it. Consider what happened this afternoon a warning, because it won't be his last attempt on your life."

"I didn't think it would be." I sighed heavily. "But I'm not walking away from her."

"Why the hell not?"

"I promised I'd help her."

"So what? People break promises all the time. She'll get over it," Knox said, his voice loaded with condescension.

"She wouldn't be in Senator Wharton's crosshairs if I didn't push her to help us."

"Senator Wharton was following her for weeks, if not months, before you made contact. From the day she read the email listing the names of all those women, her days were numbered. It was only a matter of time before he focused his attention on her. We don't need her anymore. She's more of a liability than she's worth," Knox spat out in disgust.

"I don't care. I love her. I'm not going to abandon her to that sick fuck." I'd been ignoring the emotion clawing at my chest for too long, but it was true. Somehow, someway, I had fallen for the stepdaughter of the man I hated for longer than I could recall, and there wasn't a damn thing I could do to change it.

Over the past week, I wanted to pretend it wasn't true, but being shot at brought everything into sharp focus. She could have been killed. I could have been killed, but at the time, I only cared about saving her. I would've risked my life to save hers without a second thought. It was a sobering thought, for sure.

Knox scoffed. "All the more reason to end things now. Your relationship can't go anywhere. It's toxic. Toxic for you. Toxic for her."

My fingers twisted into the bedding, and I practically ground my teeth to dust. Knox was right. I couldn't deny it, but everything about letting Langley go felt wrong. "I know."

"So end it. You got what you needed from her. Don't prolong the inevitable."

I rubbed the back of my neck. I heard the shower turn off in the bathroom. "I can't talk about this now. I need to go."

"Fine, but think about what I said."

"I will," I hedged, even though I had no intention of ending things with Langley. Things would end soon enough anyway.

"Good. What are your plans?"

"I'm cutting the trip short. We're driving back tonight."

"Send me a text when you're back in D.C."

"Bye." I hit the end button and tossed the phone on the bed next to me. Nothing made sense anymore. Against my better judgment, I had opened my heart to Langley and handed her the key to my destruction. My entire life I had waited for the right moment to ruin Senator Wharton. The need for revenge ruled every choice I made. Now, it was a distant second, if that, to having Langley in my life.

I dropped my head into my hands. I was so fucked.

"Are you okay?" Langley asked.

My eyes collided with hers. She stood at the threshold of the bedroom with wet hair and a short black robe hugging every curve of her body. She looked achingly beautiful with her face scrubbed of makeup and a gentle smile on her lips. I'd do anything to see her look at me that way every single day of the rest of my life. Too bad it was a lost cause.

I patted the bed next to me. "Come here, Langley."

She tilted her head to the side and bit her lower lip. "Am I in trouble?"

"Trouble?" I echoed.

"Yeah. You look too serious…like you're about to scold me for something."

A smile split across my face and I laughed. "That's right. Get over here."

She rolled her eyes as she crossed the room and sat down next to me.

"We need to check out of the hotel."

Her smile faded from her face. "Now?"

I rolled the cuffs back on my shirt, avoiding her gaze. "Yes. Knox believes Senator Wharton likely had something to do with what happened today. I don't want to sit around waiting for him to make his next move. We'll be safer at my place."

"You're probably right." Her voice wavered, and my stomach twisted. I didn't want her to be sad, scared, or whatever the hell she felt at that instant.

"I promise I'll take you back here or wherever you want to go when this is all over." It was an impulsive promise. The second the words left my mouth I realized I may never get the chance to take her anywhere, but if she still wanted me when this mess ended, I would do anything for her.

"You promise?" she said coyly. She placed her hand on my thigh, slowly moving it up my leg. My gaze dropped to her lips. I shouldn't touch her. I should pack our bags and be on the road back to D.C. as soon as possible, but I couldn't stop myself from tasting her again.

I slid my hands into her hair, pushing it away from her heart-shaped face, drinking her in. I didn't know how much longer we would have together. I could feel the end coming closer with every tick of the second hand. I wished I could freeze time so we could live a lifetime in the next hour.

With our eyes locked, I brushed a kiss across her parted lips. Once. Twice. Three times. She tasted like mint and something unique to her. I wanted to caress her, explore her, taste her, and consume her sighs and whimpers, locking them away like a precious memory.

I deepened the pressure, capturing her tongue with mine. Electricity sizzled through my veins. She shivered, and my muscles tightened. Instinctively, I pulled her closer, inhaling her scent. Her hands tangled in my hair, lightly scratching my scalp. Just like every time we touched, her immediate response made my head swim, and I struggled to maintain control.

In my mind, I was already calculating how fast I could get her on her back and slip off her robe. In less than thirty seconds, I could be buried inside of her one last time before we had to face reality. My mind begged me to ignore everything. Fuck Senator Wharton. Fuck my plans. Fuck the consequences.

But then I realized it was already too late. Knox had delivered the demand letter. He'd shown our hand. I had to follow this through to the end. There wasn't an easy out anymore. The realization was a cold dose of reality. Acid swirled in my gut.

I lifted my head, breaking the kiss and severing the connection. Her eyes were dilated and her lips swollen and wet, tempting me to ignore everything. I barely resisted the urge.

Her body drifted closer to me. "Why'd you stop?"

"We need to go."

"Right now?"

"Yes." I stroked her cheek with my knuckles.

She grabbed my wrist. "I'm scared," she said, her voice panicked. "I can't do this without you."

I closed my eyes and pain lanced through my chest. "I won't leave your side until this is over. Whatever happens, we're in this together."

Unfortunately, I didn't know if she'd want me by her side when this was finished.

CHAPTER TWENTY-EIGHT

Langley

"It'll just be a second. You don't have to come in with me." My hand circled the bottom of my purse as I hunted for the keys.

Archer snatched the keys out of my hand. "I don't feel comfortable letting you walk into your house by yourself."

"It's not a big deal." I glanced at the front of my house. It was already dark outside, and I wished I'd had enough forethought to leave on some lights inside my house. I pushed aside my forebodings.

If my stepdad was behind what happened today, I didn't think he'd try again so soon. Besides, he probably thought we'd stay at the hotel another night. "I'll get in and get out within ten minutes. I need to grab a couple of files for work tomorrow and a change of clothes."

Archer turned off the car ignition. "It doesn't

matter. I'm going with you. Like you said, it's only ten minutes."

I groaned. "According to Knox, Senator Wharton has more recording devices all over my home. It'd be better if you stayed in the car."

"I'm not going to say anything."

Just then, his cell phone rang. Archer dug into his pocket and pulled out his phone. "It's Knox. I have to take this," he said as he glanced at the screen. "I didn't text him when we left the hotel."

I opened the car door. "Perfect. You talk to Knox and give him an update. I'll run inside and grab what I need. I'll be back before you finish your call."

Archer's dark eyebrows slanted downward, and he pressed his lips into a firm, straight line. "Fine, but if you're not out in ten minutes, I'm going inside. I don't give a damn about those listening devices. Senator Wharton already knows about us."

"Agreed. See you in a few minutes."

I ran up the front steps of my house and opened the front door. Pausing in the entry, I flipped on the lights, and my ears strained for any unusual sounds. I scanned the narrow living room and kitchen, scouring for anything out of the ordinary. I didn't think my stepdad would show his face at my house, but after what happened today, I couldn't be too careful.

I tossed my keys and my purse on the counter and wandered the main floor. The house smelled stuffy as though it had been closed up for weeks instead of a few days. The peonies Archer gave me weeks ago were crispy, and the petals showered the kitchen countertop when I lifted the vase and placed it in the sink. Everything looked exactly as I'd left it a few days ago.

Taking a deep breath, I climbed the stairs and made my way to the small guest room I'd converted into an office last year. I flipped on the lights and took two steps into the room before I saw him.

Thomas Wharton lounged in a chair with a gun sitting on the desk. His arms were folded across his chest. Stunned, I didn't say or do anything for long, drawn out seconds. My heartbeat drummed with panic and fear. Goosebumps of terror slithered down my spine.

"What are you doing here?" I asked, wringing my hands in the hem of my shirt.

He shrugged calmly like he didn't have a care in the world. "The last time I checked, I still own this house."

"That's true." I retreated a few steps. "But you've never stopped by before."

He lifted the gun and pointed it at me. "Where do you think you're going?"

My eyes locked on the gun pointed directly at my chest. "Thomas, what's going on? What are you planning to do with that?"

"You betrayed me," he roared as he shoved the chair back and stood up. Spit showered the top of my desk. His clothes were wrinkled, and he hadn't shaved his face in at least two days. The dark circles around his eyes made him look even more sinister than normal.

I held my hands up in surrender. "I don't know what you're talking about. I didn't do anything."

"Sit down there," he said, waving the gun toward the white lounge chair adjacent to the balcony doors.

My heart squeezed painfully. "No." I shook my head. If I sat down, it would be over. I'd rather take my chances and run down the stairs or across the hall to my bedroom.

In a few strides, he crossed the room and held the gun to my scalp. "Sit."

My eyes visually ransacked the room, looking for something I could throw at him.

"Don't even try it," he warned through clenched teeth as he pressed the gun even harder into the side of my skull.

"Why are you doing this?" I pleaded softly, as I inched sideways toward the chair, my palms clammy with sweat. I wanted to flee, but I didn't have a choice. Archer said he'd come looking for me in ten minutes. Part of me wished I'd sent him home. I didn't want him to get hurt. Regardless of his promise to stand by me, this wasn't his fight. It was mine.

"Drop the fucking charade, Langley. I know you saw the email. I know you're working with Archer Black. I know you've been questioning those women and digging into their lives and mine."

"I don't know what you're talking about," I said as firmly as possible, digging my fingernails into the armrest of my chair.

In one fluid movement, my stepdad lunged and backhanded me across my face. Unprepared, my head slammed backward into the wall. Stars exploded behind my eyes and my cheek smarted with the pain of a hundred bee stings.

"Do you want to rethink your answer?" my stepdad said, looming over me, his eyes dark orbs of rage and hate.

Dazed, I didn't respond. Instead, I cupped the side of my face and shook my head slowly from side to side.

"You stupid bitch." He waved the gun in front of my face. "I took care of you and your mom. I treated you like a member of my family. I paid for your college. I let you live in my home. I gave you everything, and you're trying to repay my kindness by destroying everything I've worked for. I could lose everything. I could go to jail."

I glared at him.

The man who had been a part of my family for twelve years.

The man who I once believed could fill the hole in my heart after my dad's death.

The man whose political career I supported in too many ways to count.

I knew I needed to say something…anything. I needed more time. I needed to get out of the room. I glanced toward the balcony doors, and I saw a shadow stretching across the railing. Selfishly, I hoped it was Archer even though he'd be safer in the car. I sucked in a deep breath, striving to calm my mind and focus my thoughts. "I didn't have a choice." My voice sounded unnaturally calm. I wrapped my arms around my body, bracing myself for his reaction.

"No choice." He cocked his head to the side.

I nodded my head, but my muscles were knotted

so tightly, my head barely moved.

"What the hell does that mean?"

"You killed three women. Was I supposed to pretend it didn't happen?"

His hand moved toward me and I squeezed my eyes shut, waiting for him to strike, but it didn't happen. Instead, he grabbed me by the collar of my shirt and yanked me out of the chair. "I didn't kill them."

"You didn't?" My brows climbed my forehead in disbelief.

"No, I had more important matters demanding my time. I couldn't get away, so I hired someone to do it."

"That's the same fucking thing," I yelled as he dragged me down the hallway toward the stairs.

"You're right, but you're lucky," he said, pausing at the top of the stairs. "I plan to deal with you personally."

"Deal with me? How?" With both hands, I scratched at his wrists, struggling to release his hold on me.

He pressed me into the wall. "Suicide, just like the others. Your death won't be quite as painless, though. The others overdosed on sleeping pills or shot themselves in the head. I'm going to throw you down the stairs." He shrugged, a thin-lipped smile on his face. "I might have to snap your neck if the fall doesn't work. Who knows? I might even enjoy it."

"Nobody will believe you."

His hand slid to my neck, pressing just hard enough to restrict the airflow to my lungs. "You've been quite upset the last six months over your breakup with Brandon, haven't you? You even left a nice little note on your desk."

"The handwriting won't match mine."

He chuckled, but his eyes were hard and cold. "Oh please. That's child's play. Do you know the kind of resources a senator has at his disposal? How hard do you think it would be for me to find an expert to forge a letter or verify the authenticity of the letter?"

My hands balled into fists as fiery, sadistic anger pulsed through my body, not leaving a single cell untouched. My fingers itched to claw out his eyes. I'd never been an aggressive or physical person. I preferred words and reason, but my rational mind splintered when a smug smile crawled across his face. I wanted to kill him. Without thinking, I swung my hand toward his face, colliding with his nose in one sickening crunch. He grunted in pain and stumbled backward, cupping his nose. The gun slipped from his hand as he dropped to his knees in front of the stairway, severing any chance of escape.

"Fucking bitch," he hollered. Blood seeped like blackened lava through his fingertips.

My eyes wide with panic and my heart clobbering the inside of my ribcage, I backtracked a few steps, and then I bolted to my bedroom. Just as I reached the threshold, my stepdad's hand caught my forearm. I kicked and swung my arms, striking and scratching anything within my reach, but for every hit I landed, he landed two. There was no way I was going to win.

Within minutes, he had pinned me to the floor.

Straddling my waist, he captured my wrists in one hand. With his free hand, he held his gun to my head. Blood dribbled from his nose over his lips in a slow stream and sweat beaded at his temples. He had lost his mind.

"I'm not happy with you," he spat, his eyes narrowed into razor sharp slits, his nostrils flared.

"I can't imagine it'll be easy to explain your injuries to my mom or the police, especially if it coincides with my so-called suicide."

He squeezed my wrist so hard I thought my bones would snap. "Accidents happen all the time. I'm sure I can come up with an alternate explanation for my injuries. A car accident. Being mugged on my daily run. A slip and fall. The options are endless." He sighed wearily, as though I was the most naïve person he knew, and maybe I was. "It won't be much of a challenge."

"You won't get away with this. Archer knows everything. His brother knows everything."

"Shut up. Don't say another fucking word." His gun drilled into the side of my head. I bucked against him, but he didn't budge. I yanked my arms and twisted my hands, but his hold was too tight. My stomach churned with dread, and my heart scaled the walls of my chest to my throat, suffocating me. The edges of my vision blurred. This was it. There was nothing I could do. Inhaling what could be my final breath, I clamped my eyes shut and waited for him to pull the trigger and deliver my death.

CHAPTER
TWENTY-NINE

Archer

"Is that your car in front of Langley's house?" Knox shouted the second I answered my phone.

I glanced toward the entrance of Langley's house just as she closed the front door behind her. "Yes. Langley needed to get a few things for work tomorrow."

"Fucking hell," Knox cursed. "Don't let her go inside."

"Too late." I grabbed the gun out of the glove box. "What's going on?"

"Senator Wharton entered her house through the back door about a half an hour ago. He's still inside."

I jumped out of the car and assessed the front of her house. Just then, someone turned on the light on the second story. From the street, I saw Senator's Wharton's silhouette sitting behind a desk. "She found him. I'm going inside."

"No, you're not. You're waiting for me."

"There's not enough time."

He sighed in exasperation. "I'm less than two minutes away. Wait for me."

This was my game. I pulled Langley into the middle of this mess. She was my responsibility. There was no way I'd sit on my hands and wait for Knox. My mind kept tallying all the things that could happen to her, and I kept coming back to one fact: I was a damn fool. My pride demanded revenge against Senator Wharton, but my revenge wouldn't mean anything if I lost Langley in the process. "I'm going in through the front door," I said as I crept up the front steps. "They're upstairs. There's a balcony. You should access the house from there."

"Don't move on him until I get there," Knox warned. "It won't be long. I'm at the end of the block."

I peered over my shoulder. Dressed in black from head to toe, Knox jogged down the street with his phone glued to his ear. "I'll see you inside."

"Please tell me you remembered your gun," Knox murmured.

I turned the doorknob. Thank God she didn't lock the door when she went inside. I eased it open as silently as possible. Every squeak, rustle, or crack of the floorboard thundered in my ears. "I did," I muttered before I slipped my phone into my pocket, not bothering to disconnect the call. I pulled the slide back on my gun.

With each step, my heart felt like it would

explode inside my chest. I heard shouts, bumps, and screams. This couldn't happen. She couldn't die today. There were too many things I needed to say to her. Regardless of whether she severed all ties with me when it was over, I wouldn't begrudge her. I just wanted her to be safe and happy—whatever or however she could—even if her happily ever after didn't include me.

My back glued to the wall, I crept up the stairs one step at a time. My blood iced in my veins when I reached the top step. Senator Wharton crouched over her body, physically restraining her while he pressed a gun to the side of her head. Langley's blonde hair tangled around her face and blood trickled down her chin from a cut on her lip.

I held the gun in front of me. "Put your gun down and get the fuck away from her!"

Langley's eyes popped open, and I stepped forward. Senator Wharton paused and glanced over his shoulder. Without hesitating, he scrambled to his feet, dragging Langley with him by her hair. He wrapped his arm around her neck and aligned her back with his chest, using her body as a shield. He jammed the barrel of the gun into the side of her head.

"Ah. Here's my long lost son," Senator Wharton smiled, but his features were glacial. "I was wondering if you'd join us. We're like one big happy family, minus all of the guns, of course. We're only missing Langley's mother and Archer's mother." He angled his chin to the side. "Oh, that's right. I killed Archer's mother, so she's indisposed at the moment, but that's a minor technicality. I'm sure she's with us in spirit."

My eyes darted to Langley, and her mouth dropped open.

"That was quite ingenious of you, Langley, involving my biological son. I'm sure he didn't hesitate to join your cause."

"I didn't know," Langley mumbled so softly, I almost missed it. A tear tracked down her pale cheeks.

Senator Wharton snorted. "Archer used you, not the other way around. Like father like son. I guess you can't ignore the blood running through your veins."

"We're nothing alike," I said through clenched teeth as I took another step forward. My eyes locked on the trigger of Senator Wharton's gun, trying to anticipate his next move.

"Oh, then you're here on a heroic errand."

My eyes flickered to Langley, and then to Knox, who stood at the end of the hallway, undetected by anyone but me. "Not really."

"Then what are you doing here?" he asked.

I shrugged. "Just collecting evidence."

Senator Wharton's smile faltered momentarily. "Evidence?"

"I added some of my own listening devices and cameras to Langley's home a couple of days ago. Regardless of what happens tonight to Langley or me, your career is over."

"You still have to send it to someone, and if you're dead you can't do that," he snarled, his lips contorted into a sneer.

"It's automated. It goes to my source at the FBI

every hour on the hour." I wondered why Knox insisted on this detail. Initially, I wanted all the evidence to filter through me before he funneled it to his friends at the FBI, but now I understood his insistence.

His face twisted into a fiery rage. "Then, I have nothing to lose."

He pointed the gun at the center of my chest, and it all happened at once. Langley's eyes fluttered closed, her body sagged, and Knox pulled the trigger on his gun. Senator Wharton tumbled forward on top of Langley as the bullet pierced his shoulder. His gun dropped out of his hand, hitting the ground and skidding across the hardwood floors.

I grabbed him by his shirt and flipped him onto his back with one hand. I shoved my knee against his stomach and held the gun right between his eyes. Blood seeped from the gunshot wound, staining his wrinkled white shirt.

"The police and the FBI are on their way," Knox said, sliding his gun into the holster next to his hip. Sirens wailed down the street. "And here they are. Five minutes late."

Langley crab walked across the hallway. Her green eyes were bloodshot and swollen. Tears still stained her cheeks.

"Are you okay?" I asked. My eyes roamed every inch of her body, cataloging her injuries. A scratch on her cheekbone. Bruised wrists. But she looked like she'd be okay. Relief coursed through my veins. I could breathe again.

She nodded as she avoided my eyes. "Yes," she said, her voice faint and trembling.

"Are you hurt?" I wanted to touch her, hug her, but I couldn't do any of that until the police arrived. I didn't think Senator Wharton was capable of much, but I didn't want to take the chance either.

She swallowed and then shook her head slowly from side to side. "Not too bad. I'll be okay. Just in shock. I think."

Just then, I heard voices downstairs. "We're upstairs," I shouted.

CHAPTER THIRTY

Langley

For the last ten minutes, I had huddled inside an ambulance in front of my townhome, or the townhome I'd lived in for the last two and half years. I doubted I'd ever step foot inside again, not even to get my belongings. I didn't want anything. It was all tainted by my stepdad and his lies.

"I'm fine," I muttered for what felt like the hundredth time to the third EMT worker who asked how I was doing. He scanned my body, looking for something, probably signs of a complete and total emotional breakdown. He wouldn't find anything but a blank mask.

Numb. I felt utterly and blissfully numb. Everything happened so quickly. One instant, I was sure I'd taken my final breath, and the next, Archer stood in front of us like an avenging angel. Now my townhome and front walk were flooded with people, and I didn't think it'd be long before the media made an appearance.

Senator Wharton would be fine physically, but his career was over. I didn't know how my mom would weather the storm, but she always landed on her feet. I didn't think this time would be any different. Somehow she'd find a way to recast this whole thing to her benefit. She'd probably end up being a martyred hero.

I watched as Archer wove through the swarm of people toward me. Even after everything I learned tonight, my heart ached for him.

"Langley," he uttered, linking his hands with mine. "They're going to take you to the hospital to run some tests. I'll be there within the hour. I still have a few questions to answer. When you're done, we can go to my place."

Shocked, I yanked my hands out of his grasp. "I can't," I protested as I shook my head from side to side.

"You can't come back here either."

"I won't. I'll call Winnie, or I'll stay in a hotel near the hospital."

"No. Absolutely not," he growled. "You're staying with me until this dies down. It's going to be crazy for a while."

"I know. I just need a break from everything," I whispered.

"Does everything include me?"

I ran my tongue over my suddenly dry lips. "For now it does." I couldn't offer more of an explanation. My brain was still reeling from everything I learned tonight.

He nodded. "I should've told you Senator Wharton is my biological dad—"

"You think?" I interrupted.

"I wanted to. I really did, Langley."

I laughed, but it sounded bitter and twisted. "Then, why the hell didn't you?"

"Knox and I suspected he had something to do with my mom's death. I needed to know the truth."

My stomach lurched. "So you used me for information? That's what this whole thing was about?"

"No!"

"I'm not an idiot, Archer. Don't treat me like one."

He rubbed his hand along the side of his face. "He tossed my mom and me out of his life like we were trash. When I learned he planned to run for president, I knew I couldn't let it happen. I had to stop him."

"You mean—destroy him." I swallowed over the lump in my throat. "And me."

Remorse flashed across his face, and I knew without him saying another word that my suspicions were true. "Maybe initially, but I changed my mind. I would never hurt you. I—"

"Oh my God," I whispered, suddenly lightheaded. If I weren't sitting down, I think I would've collapsed. "You used me from the minute you met me. You planned everything. You showed up at the fundraising event to find me. You wanted to get close to Senator Wharton, and what better way to do that than to start a fake relationship with his stepdaughter and get me to trust you." I groaned as a sick sensation bubbled into my gut. "I think I'm going to be sick."

"It wasn't fake."

I scoffed. "Oh please. Do you realize what you're saying?" I ran my hands through my hair, tugging at my roots until my scalp stung. I needed something to ground me. I felt like I was going to float away. "Now I understand why you kept promising to help me and see this through until the end. It finally makes sense. It was all about getting even with him."

I hadn't realized how much faith I put in Archer and our relationship until it slapped me in the face. From the little information available about Archer, I knew he didn't do the long-term relationship thing. For some reason, I had convinced myself we'd made a real connection, and I wasn't some short-lived fling. In truth, I wasn't even a fling. I was one of the tools he used to settle a vendetta against my stepdad. I was nothing. Less than nothing.

"I wanted to protect you from him too."

"How kind. You should win an award for your compassion and your service to this country," I mocked. "You destroyed Senator Wharton. You destroyed my family. You got what you wanted. I guess congratulations on a job well done are in order."

He cradled my face between his hands, forcing me to look at him. "I know you're hurting, and you feel betrayed, but it doesn't diminish what was happening between us."

"And what was happening between us Archer?" I snapped. "Because from where I'm sitting, it looks like you used me." Each word was like a knife wound to my heart. More than anything, I wanted to offer my forgiveness and bask in the comfort of his embrace and his spicy-citrus scent. But I had been used and abused by too many people for too long. I couldn't fall back into the same pattern. I laughed, but it sounded more like a sob. "You could've told me the truth in the beginning. I would've helped you. You didn't have to pretend you wanted to be with me."

"Langley...I do want to be with you." He paused for a frozen second, then added softly. "I love you. I care about you. Give me the chance to prove myself."

"No," I screamed, feeling out of balance and slightly unhinged. "Do you think you can erase everything you did by telling me you love me? What makes you think that I still want you in my life? What we had wasn't real. Not even close. It was a lie." The minute I said those words, my heart fractured. Sobs clogged in my throat, begging to be released. I didn't want to push him away. I loved him, but I had to move on if I wanted to maintain even a shred of dignity. "Just go away, Archer. I don't want to talk to you right now."

CHAPTER THIRTY-ONE

Archer

"You look like shit."

"Thanks," I mumbled, not bothering to acknowledge Knox. I thought he was going to be out of town this weekend. Apparently, I was mistaken.

"Still no word from Langley?" Knox flopped down on the couch next to me. I wished he'd turn around and walk right out my door. Better yet, he should take that vacation he mentioned at the office yesterday.

"Nope." I stared at the television as though I was watching a riveting program. Truthfully, I didn't even know what was on the TV. Two weeks had passed since Senator Wharton tried to kill Langley, and I still hadn't heard a single word from her. Her absence left a gaping hole in my heart. I didn't know what to do. For the first time since I was a kid, I felt completely powerless.

"She still hasn't answered your calls or your

texts?"

I took a drink of my beer before answering. Two more beers and I could kiss my sobriety goodbye. I planned to remedy that problem in the next half hour. Drunk and lonely seemed infinitely more appealing than being sober and lonely. "Nope, but her number was disconnected as of this morning."

Knox plopped his feet on the top of my coffee table. On any other day, I would have objected, but today I didn't give a shit.

"Did you call her at work?"

"She took a leave of absence, or at least that's what they told me." Pain and depression from a breakup were new to me. I never cared when a woman walked out of my life permanently. When Langley told me to go away that night, I never considered for one second that she wanted me out of her life forever. I guess I was wrong. I should've listened to the underlying finality in her voice.

"Well, that's that." Knox stood up and started picking up the miscellaneous cartons of take-out that littered my counter from last night.

I waved my hand at the mess. "Don't worry about it, my cleaning lady is coming on Monday."

"Monday?" Knox glared at me. "You do realize that it's only Saturday."

"So what?" I shrugged. "The mess doesn't bother me."

"It sure as hell bothers me. It stinks like shit in here."

"Then leave. Get the fuck out of here. I don't want your company. I want to be alone," I yelled. Knox knew me better than anyone in the world, yet

235

he didn't understand why I couldn't move on. He stopped by every day, trying to draw me out of this funk. It wouldn't work. Regrets ate at my soul every hour until I felt like I was dying inch by painfully slow inch.

"You don't have a choice. This has to end today. You've ripped everyone's head off at work the past few weeks, and the entire office is avoiding you like the plague."

"So what? Once they get their year-end bonus, they'll forget about it."

Knox ripped the beer bottle out of my hand. "Don't you think you've been drinking too much?"

"Fuck you," I responded without any heat, because he was right. Drinking was the last thing someone with an alcoholic parent should do in excess.

"This is ridiculous. You're a mess, Archer. You need to move on with your life and pull yourself together. Langley isn't the only woman in the world. Call Leah. I'm sure she'd be happy to take your mind off of Langley."

I ran a shaky hand over my face. "No, dammit. I don't want to move on. Langley is the only woman I want." I'd spent my entire life shutting everyone except Knox out of my life, but somehow Langley slipped through the cracks in my armor, healing me from the inside out. I refused to let her go. I needed to make her understand what she meant to me. I wanted to marry her, build a life with her, and have children with her. It'd destroy me if I didn't find a way to make it work. I'd never get enough of her.

Her smile.

Her laugh.

The arc of her neck.

The subtle curve of her waist.

Her kindness.

I felt like I was missing part of myself.

"Fine, then let's go through your options. Have you called Langley's mom?"

I scowled at him, and my jaw muscles automatically tightened. "You know that's not an option. I'm not sure she knows where Langley is either. From what little Langley told me of her, she wasn't much of a parent." For the most part, Langley's mom had maintained a low profile since Senator Wharton was arrested. I had no idea what Langley's mom knew about my connection to her husband. So far, none of the details had leaked to the media, and I hoped it remained that way. I never wanted to acknowledge my connection to him publicly. Thank God his name wasn't on my birth certificate.

"What about her friends? Have you contacted any of them?"

"I've only met one. Winnie. My background information on her didn't extend beyond her name, Winifred Watters. I didn't spend a lot of time trying to get to know her, and her home address isn't readily obtainable."

Knox rolled his eyes. "Let me guess. You were too focused on Langley to make conversation with her friend."

"Something like that," I mumbled, remembering the night I found her at The Nine Bar. She'd looked so beautiful; I hardly glanced at Winnie.

"Here," he said. Knox reached into his pocket, pulled out a scrap of paper, and tossed it into my lap.

"What this?" I said, scanning the address, handwritten in block letters.

"Winnie's address. Langley's been living there for the past two weeks. During the week, Winnie leaves for work at eight thirty, and she doesn't come home until after six, except on Fridays. She goes to happy hour with her co-workers or friends. Langley hasn't joined her since the Senator Wharton scandal. Winnie's weekend schedule varies."

"What about Langley? What has she been doing?"

"She doesn't leave Winnie's house often."

A spasm of pain ripped through my chest. "How did you get all of that information?"

Knox smirked. "I have connections."

I stuffed the handwritten address into my pocket. "Why didn't you give this to me earlier?"

"Because I thought you'd be over her by now, but instead of snapping out of this, you're getting more and more pathetic with every passing day," he said with amusement.

I shoved him in the shoulder. "It's not funny. This whole thing isn't funny."

Knox chuckled. "That's where you're wrong. This whole scenario is insanely funny. You've only cared about making money for as long as I can remember. Now, you've spent the last two weeks moping over a woman."

I grabbed my keys and wallet off the coffee table. "Can you lock up when you leave?"

"Where are you going?"

"I'm going to find Langley and make her talk to me."

"Like that?" he said, eyeing my wrinkled clothes.

I opened my front door. "I don't want to waste any more time." And I didn't. I refused to believe I'd lost my chance to be with Langley.

"At least drink some coffee before you go."

"I'll stop on my way."

CHAPTER THIRTY-TWO

Langley

"Thanks for meeting me. I think it's time we talk about how we're going to handle this incident. We need to make a plan to move forward," my mom said as I walked into the intimate dining room.

For the first time in two weeks, she called me last night and asked me to join her for lunch. Initially, I was surprised she had picked such a popular restaurant, but she quickly explained that she arranged for us to meet in a private room.

"I agree," I said as I slipped into the chair across from my mom. She looked as immaculately groomed as ever. She wore an emerald green pantsuit with gold buttons. Her hair was coiffed into an elegant bun and her makeup was expertly applied.

"Did you come in through the back door?" she asked.

"Yes." I tucked my hair behind my ears. "The calls from the press have died down the last few days."

"That's good. It's been a couple of weeks, and we've both refused to comment on what happened, so that's expected."

"Right. I think they have most of the relevant details from the police and FBI." My mom's lips pressed into a narrow line and she jerked her head to the side. I grabbed her hand from her lap and squeezed it. It was cold to the touch. "How are you holding up? Are you okay?"

She slipped her hand from mine and picked up the white linen napkin on her plate and placed it in her lap. "I'm fine, Langley. Better than I have been over the last two weeks."

Guilt speared through my chest. Too caught up in my turmoil, I'd been avoiding her, but in my defense, this was the first time she asked to see me since I was discharged from the hospital. Even in the hospital she only peeked her head into my room for a few minutes before she excused herself.

"That's good," I muttered.

She took a sip of her ice water, but her eyes never left mine. "I met with Senator Wharton's legal team today. We decided how to shape his defense."

The edges of my vision blurred and my blood froze in my veins. "You're helping his attorneys?"

She tilted her head to the side. "Of course I am. You didn't leave me with much of a choice."

"He tried to kill me," I hissed as I clutched the folds of my dress, twisting the material between my fingers.

"What do you expect me to do?"

"Stand by me. Support me. Your daughter. Not him."

Her lips twisted into something resembling a sneer. "Why should I do that? You ruined my life. You have never given a second thought about how your actions affect me. Not once."

"My actions?" Baffled, I shook my head. "What did I do to you?"

"You stole your dad from me. Now you've successfully ruined my marriage with Senator Wharton. So here I am, alone again."

There were so many things wrong with that statement. I could hardly form a response. "I didn't steal dad. He died of a drug overdose."

She snorted. "You're wrong. He abandoned me long before he died. From the moment you took your first breath, you were the only thing he cared about. He loved you so much he didn't have anything left for me. He didn't care what I wanted or needed. His whole life revolved around you. I went from being his everything to an afterthought in the blink of an eye."

My eyes flared. Her words were senseless…unhinged. A normal person wouldn't interpret a father-daughter relationship that way. "Mom, he loved you," I said, because words escaped me.

"No. You're wrong. He wanted a divorce. He planned to leave me. He didn't want me anymore. He only wanted you, and now you've managed to ruin my second marriage too. I shouldn't have taken you with me after your father died. I should've left you with your father's sister. She wanted you. She loved you."

My vision spun like I had vertigo, and I thought I'd be sick. There was always an invisible wall between my mom and me. Now I knew why. She hated me. She viewed me as her competition, not her child. "Thomas would've killed me. Doesn't that mean anything to you? He held a gun to my head. I closed my eyes, believing my life was over. If it weren't for Archer and his brother—"

"Archer Black?" The name rolled off her lips like poison. "I warned you to stay away from him, but you wouldn't listen."

"You warned me?" I shook my head in disbelief. "No. You never said anything about him."

"Who do you think left those notes on your car?"

I shuddered as the confession left her lips. "I assumed they were from Thomas. I never dreamed you would do something like that," I said, but the words were barely audible.

"Well, I did. I put them on your car. I couldn't have you around that man. Thomas said he'd take care of it. He wanted me to stay out of it, but I couldn't." She shook her head from side to side. "I knew why he wanted you."

"What do you mean?" I said, sliding my phone out of my pocket and dialing Winnie's home number while keeping the phone concealed in my lap. She was meeting her sister for lunch, so the call would go to voicemail, which was perfect. I'd have a recording of the entire conversation.

"He was bitter because Thomas didn't want anything to do with him."

My stomach dropped. "You know Archer is his

son?" I whispered.

She rearranged the silverware next to her plate, avoiding my eyes. "Of course I did. Thomas and I don't have secrets. We're a team."

The blood rushed out of my face as the implications of her words knifed through my heart. "You know about those women and you don't care?"

She shrugged. "Grow up, Langley. Men have needs. They have affairs. It doesn't mean anything. Even your saintly dad had affairs. Those women knew the score."

"Those women?" I questioned. "What's wrong with those women? They didn't do anything to you."

She rolled her eyes. "Those women were escorts. They were well paid for their services. They made a deal. They can't change their mind after the fact and blackmail their clients for more money later."

"They weren't even eighteen years old. Did you know that?"

"Who cares? They're trash," she snapped.

"He had three of them killed." I couldn't mask the revulsion in my voice.

"He did what he had to do. I support his decisions. We have the same end goal."

"And what's that?"

"He's going to be the next president, and I'm going to be the next first lady." She smiled serenely like she actually believed it could still happen.

"I think it's a little late for that. Don't you?"

She rested her elbows on the edge of the table and leaned forward. "No, because you're going to help us clear up this little misunderstanding."

"There wasn't a misunderstanding. Thomas intended to kill me. He held a gun to my head. He threatened to throw me down the stairs and then break my neck."

"Don't be so dramatic. He was just trying to scare you. He wouldn't have killed you."

"You weren't there. You don't know what happened." I folded the napkin in my lap and set it on top of my plate. "I don't think we have anything more to talk about." My heart was battered, bruised, and bloody. I didn't know the woman sitting across from me. I was obviously in denial when I thought she cared about me.

She grabbed my wrist, and her nails dug into my flesh. "No. I'm not done talking to you. You're going to sit down and sign a sworn affidavit claiming Senator Wharton was at your home per your request. Archer and his brother mistakenly believed he was an intruder and shot him."

"No," I yelled, shaking my head back and forth. "I won't lie to save Thomas. He's a murderer and a liar. Besides, I already talked to the police and the FBI. I can't change my testimony now. They won't believe me."

"You can and you will."

"No."

"I can make your life uncomfortable if you don't agree."

Laughing at the irony of her words, I twisted my arm out her grasp. "You don't have any power. Nobody wants anything to do with Thomas, and you're tainted by association. Your friends won't talk to you. The members of his party can't distance themselves from the Wharton name fast enough," I snarled through clenched teeth, venom dripping from every syllable of every word. "It's over. You don't even control my trust fund anymore."

She lurched forward, struggling to grab my arm again. "You can't leave."

"Don't touch me," I said, carefully articulating each word as I slid out of my chair. "I have nothing to say to you. You're dead to me." My voice cracked on the last word, because it was the absolute truth. I never wanted to see her again. I lost my dad over ten years ago. Now, I didn't have a mother either. Maybe I never did.

The realization lay heavy on my heart. I had to get out of there before I shattered into a million unrecognizable pieces. Rushing across the room, I pushed open the heavy wooden doors separating us from the rest of the customers in the restaurant.

"Langley, wait. I didn't excuse you."

I ignored her, moving as fast as possible without breaking into a full run. I had entered the restaurant through the back door as my mom instructed. She wanted us to avoid any prying eyes. Unfortunately, I didn't go unnoticed as I raced to the front door.

Even through the tears blurring my vision, I saw dozens of eyes following me as I wove through the tables. I recognized a few faces. Thankfully, they were all too stunned to comment on my behavior. When I reached the door, I wiped the tears from my face and opened the door with as much dignity as I could muster under the circumstances.

CHAPTER THIRTY-THREE

Archer

Nobody answered the door. At first, I thought Langley was avoiding me. I peeked into the front windows before I realized no one was inside. I refused to go home until I talked to her, so I sat down on the front step of Winnie's townhome.

Less than five minutes later, I spotted Langley running down the street, her golden hair streaming out behind her. She didn't see me yet. She focused her gaze on the sidewalk. When she reached the front step of Winnie's townhome, she halted mid-stride, and her eyes locked on me. Her blood drained from her face, and she swayed on her feet. For a split second, I thought she'd faint.

"Archer?" she said, her voice shaky and a little raspy.

I jumped to my feet and ran down the steps to meet her. Her eyes were red-rimmed, and mascara streaked her cheeks. Seeing her upset knocked the wind out of me. I felt like I'd been punched in the gut. "Langley, what's going on? Are you okay?"

New tears welled in her eyes and her hands curled into fists. "Dammit, Archer. Why can't you leave me alone? I can't do this today."

"No." I took one step closer. Close enough that I could smell her, breathe her in, and feel the heat radiating from her body. It took every ounce of willpower in my body to stop myself from pulling her into my arms. She wasn't ready. "I'm not leaving. I need to talk to you."

She wiped the tears from her face with the back of her hand. "Not today. I just can't."

"Langley…" I said, and then took a shuddering breath. Her eyes landed on mine, and for the first time in my life, I was scared.

Scared I lost her forever.

Scared she'd never forgive me.

Scared she'd never look at me with love in her eyes again.

I tucked a strand of her hair behind her ear. "For the past two weeks, I've replayed every moment of our time together, wishing I had made different decisions. Wishing I never knew my biological father's name. Wishing we'd met under different circumstances, but I keep coming back to the same thing."

"What's that?"

"I wouldn't change a single thing because it brought you into my life. I love you, Langley, and I'm dying inside thinking you'll never give me another chance. I need you—"

Before I could finish, she wrapped her arms around my neck and buried her face into me. "My mom knew about everything. She didn't care what my stepdad tried to do to me. She wrote those notes. She doesn't care about me. She hates me."

"Shh," I murmured, snaking my arms around her waist and rocking her back and forth. "It'll be okay. I'm here." Questions rushed to the tip of my tongue. I wanted answers, but more than answers, I wanted to be close to her. Hold her. Support her. Love her. Be anything she wanted me to be.

"I feel so alone," she mumbled between sobs. "She never wanted me. She blamed me for everything."

"You're not alone. You have me."

Her body turned into stone in my arms before she relaxed again. "Do I?" she said softly, as though the thought wasn't meant for my ears. I could hear the disbelief warring with optimism in her voice.

She lifted her head cautiously and gazed at me. I framed her face with my hands, drinking in her sea-green eyes, letting her see me. The real me, not the mask I presented to the world...just the man who loved her. "I know you're angry and you don't think you can trust me. I get it. But I'll make it up to you. I promise."

I kissed the still damp trail of tears tracking down her face, leisurely making my way to her lips. I kissed her slowly, lovingly at first, but it didn't take more than a few seconds for it to evolve into a sensuous kiss. I poured every emotion and ounce of love into that kiss, hoping she'd forgive me. Hoping she'd give me a second chance. Hoping she'd let me be part of her life…forever.

And then she started to cry.

I lifted my head. "What's wrong?"

"You really love me, don't you?" she whispered between sobs.

"I do. I really do."

"I love you too."

"Even though Senator Wharton is my father—"

She ran her finger over my lips, silencing me. "I don't care about that. He doesn't matter. Not anymore."

Just like that, the anxiety that had become my constant companion over the last two weeks vanished. Her simple declaration mended everything I never realized was broken inside of me. I lifted her up, wrapping her legs around my waist, breathing in her light floral scent, giving thanks for everything that brought her into my life…even the man I refused to acknowledge for most of my life. With Langley at my side, I could do anything, be anyone. I didn't need hate or revenge to fuel me or shape my future. Love was so much more powerful.

"Where are we going?"

"My place. Our place. Together."

"You're pretty sure of yourself."

"No, I'm being proactive. I'm not giving you the opportunity to run away again."

EPILOGUE

Eight months later...

Langley

"Are you ready for your big day?" Archer handed me a cup of coffee as I walked into the kitchen.

"I'm nervous, but I'm ready," I answered honestly.

Archer wrapped his arms around me, and I rested my head against his chest, listening to the solid drum of his heart. Six months ago, Archer and I moved to Los Angeles. With the scandal surrounding my stepdad and the fallout with my mom looming over us, both of us decided we needed a fresh start. I missed Winnie every day, but I didn't regret the decision for a second, and maybe one day she'd agree to move here. I asked her at least once a week.

My stepdad was in jail, and my mom testified against him in exchange for immunity. She tried to contact me once, but I never returned her call. I'd never forgive her for taking his side, or the things she said the last time I saw her. As far as I was concerned, neither of them were part of my family.

Archer started a west coast division of Black Investments, and I enrolled in acting classes. At first, I was nervous I couldn't live up to my dad's legacy, but as the days and weeks rolled by, I realized I didn't care. I had the opportunity to live my dream with the man I loved cheering me on, and that was all that mattered. His love and constant support banished all the shadows in my life, and even if I didn't make it in Hollywood, I still had Archer.

Archer brushed a kiss on the crown of my head. "Don't worry, the job is yours. You're a natural, and the part is perfect for you."

"They might not agree with you."

"Well, then they're stupid."

"You have to say that. You're my fiancé." Just saying the word fiancé made my heart skip a beat.

His arm tightened around my waist and he nuzzled my neck. "Mm...I like being your fiancé. Will you be home by six?"

"I should be."

"Great. Knox is in town, and we're going to go out and celebrate the beginning of your new career."

I tilted my chin up, and his dark eyes zeroed in on me. "I thought Knox was doing some undercover hush-hush job?"

"Apparently, it's over now. He texted me this morning telling me he'd be in L.A. this afternoon."

My eyes flickered to the side. Even after all this time, I still felt uneasy around Knox. On the surface, he gave the impression of being easy-going, but his quick smiles didn't fool me. A dark intensity lurked under his veneer of charm, but Archer loved him, and that was good enough for me. "Sounds perfect."

Archer grinned. "You're still uncomfortable around him."

"No," I said automatically, shaking my head.

"Your acting skills may fool other people, but I can see right through you."

I sighed. "Okay, maybe a little."

"He likes you."

"He does?" I said, scrunching up my nose.

"Yes. You're part of our family."

"Family?" I chewed on my lower lip. "I like the sound of that." And I did. After my dad died, I never felt like I belonged to anyone. I was always on the outside looking in, waiting for someone to notice me and want me.

Archer changed all of that.

"So do I," he whispered against my lips.

Acknowledgments

Thank you for purchasing my book. I can't even begin to put to words what it means to me to be able pursue my love of writing.

To my husband, who puts up with a lot of craziness from me so I can get these stories out of my head.

To Limitless Publishing for continuing to support me, and Rachel Whitwam for squeezing me into her editing schedule.

Finally to Hype PR, all the bloggers, readers, and reviewers: I couldn't do this without you!

About the Author

After spending years practicing law and running a real estate development company with her husband, Lisa decided to pursue her dream of becoming a writer and she must confess that inventing characters is so much more fun than writing contracts and legal briefs. A native of Colorado, she lives with her husband and three children in Denver. When she isn't managing the chaos of raising three children and owning her own business, she can be found reading or writing a book or tinkering in her garden.

Facebook:
https://www.facebook.com/lcardiff11

Twitter:
https://twitter.com/lcardiff_author

Website:
http://lisacardiff.com/

Goodreads:
https://www.goodreads.com/author/show/7692079.
Lisa_Cardiff